BELOW THE GREEN POND

GREEN POND

JANE WALLER

ILLUSTRATED BY MICHAEL SPARK

GLIS-GLIS PUBLISHING

9510000034168

I dedicate the book to my husband, Michael Vaughan-Rees

First published 1982 by Abelard Shuman Limited

Published 2012 by Glis-Glis Publishing

British Library Cataloguing in Publication Data

Waller, Jane

Below the green pond.

1.Title

823'.914[J]   PZ7

ISBN 978-0-9573170-2-4

1. Contents

They loved the green pond. It was their secret place,
and they knew everything about it.

PART 1

1

THE POND

The pond was large and round and green, and when the sun shone onto it, the greenness glowed with a strange intensity. From afar, this appeared as a carpet of moss, but as you got closer, you could see that in certain places, the green thickened into a brown blanket covering a hidden depth. Towards the edges of the pond, the green thinned out, faintly tinged with yellow. In places, it parted completely to show clear shiny areas which looked friendly and inviting. But at the very centre of the pond, where the pale water crowfoot pressed their delicate white flowers against the surface, and where the sun pierced the filmy skin, a different kind of green was reflected, seeming to come from the deep; a mysterious brightness, diffused with an uncanny glow that belonged to no part of the world above.

"No-one is to go anywhere near the pond today! Do you hear?"

Owen and his twin sister, Bethan, looked across the breakfast table at their Father. His command startled them, and the look on his face meant 'very serious.'

Owen nodded, then looked back at his sister. She'd already raised one dark eyebrow, quick as a flash, in that special, questioning way that was a language they used between them. They'd promised to bring some frogspawn from the pond to take to school the following day. The rest of their class would be relying on them.

"And the reason why," their Father continued, "is because we're testing the new Vertical Take-off 'Fighter 1-11' today. There'll be sound barriers cracking louder than pistol-shots; far too dangerous for you to be anywhere near."

"OK, Dad," Bethan said, in a way that meant she had her fingers crossed beneath the table.

"OK," Owen said, his fingers also crossed tightly, the way he knew hers would be.

"As long as we go right now," Bethan said, once they'd finished a hurried bowl of cornflakes and a piece of toast, "then we'll easily make it there and back long before Dad even starts on the testing."

"And I know exactly where the frogspawn will be, Bethan, – just where it was last year, and the year before."

They were soon away from their small Welsh village, dodging along the side of the field towards the thicket that led to the air-field nearby. They skirted through an area of woodland above the grassy bank that sloped downwards to the pond.

They loved the green pond. It was their secret place, and they knew everything about it. Bethan quickly left him to look among the shallows, where water and weeds gave way to a series of low mud-banks. Owen let her do her own thing; she wouldn't find any frogspawn in that part, but he knew Bethan liked the shallows best, where the ground was pock-marked with small holes and tiny trails where various feet had been. These either lead back into the pond, or to other hiding places where bull-rush, purple loosestrife and red hemp agrimony pressed together to make a dense covering.

Owen made his way round to the furthest part where the pond deepened considerably, and tall branches of two willows drooped sadly, their frond-like ends trailing aimlessly into the water. In the darkness of their roots, he knew mud cliffs sheered steeply beneath the surface, hiding larger holes and long, interconnected burrows. Here, he might discover the spawn, carefully woven between the reedy leaves of the iris, which held giant buds already swelling on their stems. These fringed the grassy bank that sloped upwards through the thorn bushes towards where the dangerous runway began.

Owen lay on his stomach and slithered as silently as he could towards the edge. There he could stare into all the green stuff swirling around like a giant soup and watch the bubbles seething to the surface in the sun. And if he was quick, he could catch the plop of a water-vole diving into the water. But he never saw one. They were too quick and secretive. Now he started to search around for some spawn, but could find none in that part of the pond. But what he did see was a newt, right under his gaze, sitting on a stone. They stared at one another for a moment before the newt gave a flick with his tail and darted away.

It must have been my glasses that frightened him, Owen thought sadly. They always scare everyone away. His thick pebbly glasses were all right if you were Owen looking through them because they made the world much clearer, but to the world ... and probably the newt ... they must make him appear rather strange. That was why his school-mates called him 4-eyes Owen; and they were right really, because when he looked at himself in the mirror as he was cleaning his teeth, he did look pretty 'goggly'. But without the glasses he could see nothing at all.

Being nearly blind made Owen feel distant from everyone else. Bethan, who didn't need glasses at all, belonged to the 'gang'. But as hard as she tried to get them to accept her brother, they refused to let him in. They treated him as if he was there almost by accident, and he'd grown so used to this now that he had retreated into a small private world of his own where he rode a fast red car at the front of the race, or showed famous collectors his specimens of rare black beetles he'd discovered in the jungle. Best of all he was, like his Dad – a Test Pilot with briefcase and smart uniform, walking over the tarmac towards the brand new fighter plane he was about to test out. Owen wished he too could be a Test Pilot when he grew up, but knew that would be impossible with his eyesight.

'Are you paying attention Owen?' Ratty their Maths master would yell, and Owen would have to make an emergency landing on the air-strip in Peru that was really too small for the large plane he was flying, and return to Maths again.

Because of his day-dreaming, Owen's reports at school were, as you can imagine, poor. Bethan was miles above him in most subjects, while Owen didn't feel very clever at anything, except perhaps at Natural History, because sometimes in those lessons you were allowed to look through the microscope at things. And suddenly, when you adjusted the lens correctly for your eye, they would get very magnified and clear in front of you. Once, when he and Bethan had been asked to bring back a jam-jar of water from their secret pond, he'd looked at a sample of the water set carefully on glass slides. The results had been astonishing. Those small droplets of water had yielded up hundreds of small wriggling things. There were tiny flea-like ones with feathery legs, round pod-like creatures with tufts of hair sprouting from the tops of their heads, and other things that one could only call 'squiggly-wigglies'. Mr Allbright, the Natural History master, had named and drawn them on the whiteboard. Everyone had copied the drawings – after a fashion – and written their complicated Latin names in large letters beneath. Owen did his very carefully and, getting full marks, had for once become top of the class ... even higher than Bethan. Mr Allbright had been delighted, and a special bond had grown between them from that day on. The others thought Owen must have cheated somehow, and they jeered at him. But because of this event Owen had felt 'pretty nearly happy'. And this was why he and Bethan had been asked to bring in some frogspawn to watch. And he wasn't going to let Mr Allbright down.

Owen balanced his jam-jar on the bank beside him and sat under a stumpy thorn bush for a while before joining Bethan. He listened to the rooks that flapped and cawed noisily over the tree tops. The croak of frogs made him look forward to the time when the tadpoles would hatch, for the thing he liked most about the pond was watching them wriggling amongst the weed. He often wondered how they came out of their jelly, and then he fell to wondering what was underneath all the green slimy pond weed, and what made the bubbles come up one behind the other. They were a bit frightening the way they travelled up from the ooze at the bottom, because at the surface they either exploded or collected in large frothy masses around the reeds. And where they exploded, they brought up a pond smell from the deepest darkest depth.

Just then, two things happened in quick succession – and one of them completely changed Owen's life. First, he heard a moorhen splash into the pond and swim strongly towards the deeper part of the pond where the sun made it glow. Then, a split second later, he experienced an ear-splintering double bang that seemed to charge into the sides of his head and numb his ears. A gleaming slice of silver streaked upwards overhead. Then something very strange happened. The world as Owen saw it through his pebbly glasses disappeared completely as both lenses cracked simultaneously, shattering into a thousand fragments. Looking through the kaleidoscope of these prisms as they crazed into smaller and yet smaller pieces, Owen felt he was shrinking uncontrollably.

"Help! What's happening? Help me someone, help!" But Owen's voice seemed to dip away from him, becoming very faint and small. Instinctively, he wrenched the broken glasses from his face and flung them aside. At the same time he forced himself to open his eyes wider. But the strong rays of the sun filled his whole head with yellow light. He cried out again, but his voice grew even fainter. He tried to get up but tripped over the jam-jar, fell, and began rolling over and over through blades of grass, which had grown as tall as trees. The jar seemed to be getting bigger all the time as they tumbled down the bank to the water's edge. Faster and faster they rolled as the spinning in Owen's head increased. Then he and the jar plunged at great speed into the depth of the green pond.

*What should he do? He must stop turning. He decided to
stretch his arms sideways and open his fingers wide
to make himself less streamlined...*

2

BELOW THE GREEN POND

The sinking sensation seemed to go on forever. He could feel that his eyes were tightly shut and his face screwed up into a frown, but the rest of his body was spinning out of control. He clutched at his head to try and think. His fingers felt his hair streaming out behind. What should he do? He must stop turning. He decided to stretch his arms sideways and open his fingers wide to make himself less streamlined. This worked well. He could feel his hair fold back slightly and fall closer to the top of his head. After a while the spinning stopped and he felt himself descending steadily. This falling sensation made him a little seasick, but it was quite enjoyable; rather like falling asleep ... or was he drowning? He was sure it was water around him, as it was the same kind of wateryness he felt when he submerged himself in the bath, or when his mother kindly rinsed shampoo from his head with a jug of water; but instead of being too hot or too cold as it usually was, this wateryness was different. Thicker, smoother and very gentle as it touched his cheeks and eyelids; and so warm, cosy and just right, it was like that other kind of feeling you have waking in the morning in the warmth of the sheets. He decided to open his eyes.

It was then he recognised them; those bubbles! Rushing past him in a great hurry, each jostling the one above, and all in their perfect lines ... only there was something different; they were *huge*. Shiny, smooth and so, so rounded. As each bubble spiralled its way up, bright colours – pink, mauve, orange, yellow – were reflected on its surface from a strange glowing light. Falling gently now, Owen could reach out with his hands and touch one as it slid past. How slippery it was. It wobbled away from his touch, spoiling the line so that a new sequence was formed in a slightly different direction until the bubbles righted themselves.

Owen smiled with joy. As he did so, he became aware of two important things. One was that for the first time in his life he had seen and touched something he felt was utterly perfect. The second was even more wonderful. When he smiled and spread the edges of his mouth upwards, he no longer felt the uncomfortable rims of his glasses-frames rubbing against his cheeks. When he put his hands to his face, he found that his glasses had gone, yet he could see as clearly and precisely as he could with his glasses on. No! He could see more clearly. This must be a kind of miracle, he thought, like what happens in my day-dreams, only real. In fact it feels more real than everyday life. But just then he reached the bottom.

The bottom of the pond wasn't at all how he imagined it to be. It wasn't muddy and squelchy like the mud in a puddle, or even slippery and slimy as it was at the shallow end of the pond; instead it was soft, slightly fluffy, with smaller particles suspended in the water just above it. Owen looked at his feet, expecting to see a mark where he had landed, but there wasn't one. He must be very light, almost weightless. He certainly felt lighter. He could move his arms round freely in wave-like ripples. He decided to jump as high as he could and land again to test the ground. Bending his knees and pushing down with his arms, he sprang upwards. This took far less energy than expected, and sent him soaring for a while before he landed gently on the soft sediment, which drifted all about him like snowflakes in the wind. He looked around. The mud floor rose and fell in sculpted mounds, undulating rather like pictures of the moon's surface, but without rough craters or jagged edges. Everything was gentle and smooth.

And then suddenly Owen was afraid. He felt the same kind of isolation that the moon-pictures gave him. What did it all mean? He had landed at the bottom of the pond without sinking into the mud; he was weightless and could see without his glasses. What had really happened? He thought about the bubbles. Why were they so immense if it didn't mean that he was somehow smaller than a bubble? If the bubbles were so big, he must be minutely small. Maybe only just visible to the naked eye … rather like one of those squiggly-wigglies under the microscope. Perhaps he had even turned into a squiggly-wiggly? No, thank goodness, he hadn't. Those were his knees and shorts, his pullover and shoes. He sighed with relief. But the sound that escaped from his mouth was unlike any above the pond. It took more effort getting out of his lungs; then shot away from him at great speed, so he was instantly alone again except for the soft rhythmic plopping of the bubbles. Could anyone have heard him … the squiggly-wigglies perhaps … or anyone else for that matter? Or was he alone at the bottom of the pond? If there were other things, what would they think of him? He thought he saw a dark shape loom up and go past him quietly and quickly, but he wasn't sure. The light from above penetrated only a little way through the gloom. For a long time he sat and worried about being at the bottom of a pond and then slowly he began to cry. All the crying noises came out altered and were soaked up by the listening pond as if it was hungry for sound: even the tears on his face were instantly diluted, melting into the surrounding water. He felt lonely and afraid like that time he was at the seaside when they had tried to make him swim. His glasses had been left behind in case they floated away and he couldn't see the shore. How he wished he could have somebody with him now. How he wished Bethan were here.

Owen was about to cry harder, when he heard a tittering laugh behind him. He stopped crying immediately, and was about to reach into his pocket for a handkerchief to dry his eyes, when he thought how silly that would be, and laughed instead. The laughter came out as a delightful gurgling sound, like bath-water going out or a bubbling brook. It was so funny it made him laugh harder. In fact he laughed till he cried. Then he stopped crying and in the quietness heard the tittering sound again, this time from in front of him. He peered through the gloom. Coming towards him was a creature he recognised at once from Mr Allbright's drawing on the whiteboard. It was a beautiful squiggly-wiggly.

Her legs were neatly arranged in pairs down the soft part of her body.
They were leaf-like except for the last two, which
Owen thought she must use for walking.

3

THE SQUIGGLY-WIGGLIES

She was roughly the same size as Owen. Her eyes were set high on the side of her head and ringed with little petal-like structures resembling a daisy. Her mouth was opened in a slight 'O'. She moved towards him in a kind of dance: a hop, a pause, a turn through an angle, then another hop. As she moved, she waved her two double-branching arms, which were plumed with the most beautiful crimson tufts of hair. Her legs were neatly arranged in pairs down the soft part of her body. They were leaf-like except for the last two, which Owen thought she must use for walking. The most amazing thing about her was her shell, which was transparent so that he could see everything that was going on inside! She had a green middle, and Owen guessed that she had just eaten something green; he could see her heart pounding away at a fantastic rate. He could even see the blood circulating around her body. She used her strong arm-like muscles for swimming, and on her back carried a transparent pouch in which some eggs were placed as neatly as in a bird's nest.

They both looked at one another in amazement, until the squiggly-wiggly grew embarrassed and blushed throughout her body, quickly closing her mouth. Owen felt he had been particularly rude to stare at her … and through her … so he smiled. "Sorry," they said at the same time, and the concentric rings of their "sorries" met and circled through one another in the water. This made them both laugh, so they were soon surrounded by the minutest silvery bubbles that caught the light and entranced the atmosphere ... and made them both feel easier.

"My name's Owen ... How do you do," he added politely.

"My name's Sedilla. Order Crustacea: family Cladocera or water-flea, and species Sida Crystallina," she answered, tittering again.

Owen was about to remark on the length of all her names, when another water-flea, dancing through the water in the same series of hops, angles and pauses, swam up excitedly and shouted at a third flea swimming behind, "Oh look Daphnia, quickly. A new thing has just fallen into the pond!" She motioned with her feathery arms towards where Owen stood, once more shy and embarrassed.

"Do shut up, both of you," ordered Sedilla angrily. "He's not a 'thing', he's Owen. He's just introduced himself to me ... and what's more, he's mine. I found him first. He fell right past me and I followed him down." The others tittered nervously and blew small pearl-like bubbles out of their mouths.

"But what is he? He is a 'thing' isn't he? How strange he is. I've never seen anything quite like him before, have you, Faluffel?"

"No, no," squeaked Faluffel, "do introduce us quickly, please. We don't want to steal him, just share him. We saw him fall as well. We didn't mean to be rude."

"All right then, but you mustn't call him a 'thing', when he is definitely a ... definitely a ... anyway, he is obviously sensitive to your remarks. You've made him quite embarrassed, poor thing; I mean not 'thing'. What are you?" she asked, as the others burst into giggles again.

"Well," answered Owen, smiling shyly, "I'm a boy."

"There you are," said Sedilla, knowingly. "That's what I thought. He's not a 'thing', he's a boy, and his name's Owen. But what species are you? It's all very well giving your name; we all have names; but when you're introduced to someone new in Pond-life, you have to be a wee bit formal and give your genera, class, or species, or you wouldn't know where you were with anyone, would you?"

"No, I suppose not," answered Owen. "But it's very difficult to pronounce Latin, let alone understand it."

Sedilla grew stern. "There's no reason at all to be scared by strange Greek or Latin words. The names are quite harmless to pronounce if you do it slowly; and they're of great assistance in telling you more about their owners."

"Oh, all right then," said Owen, rather humbled. "In that case, I suppose I'm a member of the family Homo Sapiens. A small Homo Sapiens."

"Ah, Man the Wise. A wise Boy-man," said Sedilla, translating. "He must be still in his larval stage," she said aside to the others. "Well, you must be very clever indeed to have such a name. You'll have to teach us a lot of new things. Owen, these are my two sisters Daphnia and Faluffel; both from the same family and genera as myself."

"How do you both do?" asked Owen politely.

"Very well, thank you," they both squeaked in excited high-pitched voices, crowding round him, pushing him gently with their noses and nudging him playfully with their arms. "And you?"

"Very well, thank you," replied Owen, realizing he had never felt so well in all his life. "And very happy now I've met you."

How friendly they all were. How delicate their movements and how sweet the minute pearl-bubbles that escaped from their mouths when they spoke. Faluffel was the prettiest. Her head sloped in a kind of horn on top. Beneath the broad protruding forehead, her daisy-like eyes sparkled and twinkled, huge and wide. There was a slight blush to her cheeks and she looked nervous and very young.

Daphnia was an exceedingly large water-flea. Her chest seemed to have settled onto her stomach, which curved round it to end in a spiky tail, and she trailed her spiky arms through the water in expansive gestures as she flounced along.

"Please, why have you come?" she asked, wriggling with curiosity.

"It's perfectly obvious why he's here," interrupted Faluffel. "He's a guest arrived specially for my wedding, aren't you, Owen?"

"Yes, that's right," Owen answered quickly, feeling at once very important.

"And do please tell us where you come from," said Sedilla.

"I come from above the pond."

"Above the Pond!" they all echoed together. "What, beyond the Green?"

"Ooh!" said Faluffel. "Then he must have fallen right through the water-skin. Do please tell us what it's like and what your purpose is there?"

Owen wasn't quite sure that he could explain a Boy's purpose. He'd always wanted to know the answer to that himself. As for what it was like above the Green, it would be a long job describing it to such creatures.

"Well up there," he started, "are earth and sky, hills and houses, traffic and roads ... oh dear ..." He saw the blank looks on their faces as their great efforts to understand failed them at every attempt.

I must do better than this, he thought. "And there are others like me, both bigger and smaller, and school and the vertical take-off 'Fighter 1-11' ..." he was talking faster now and growing more desperate ... "oh, help ... and birds, the rain and sun..."

Luckily, at the mention of the last three names, their faces lit up.

"Oh yes," said Sedilla, "We know all about the birds, the kingfisher, the heron and the pied wagtail. We like the birds. They eat up the giant Sticklebacks and the larvae of insects which eat us."

"Yes, and we know about the rain too," said Daphnia. "It falls loudly onto the Green, sending up huge plops, and refreshes the Pond with new water. We love the rain."

"And as for the Sun," concluded Faluffel, "We worship the Sun. The Sun is our god." They all lowered their heads and bowed their faces in reverence.

"When the Sun shines upon the Green," said Sedilla softly, "everything glows with a strange light."

"And everything seethes and drinks in the heat," whispered Daphnia.

"And the Bottom ferments too, causing our bubble-toys to form and be released," said Faluffel.

"We love the Sun. We love the Sun," they all chorused, squiggling and wriggling in a practised flea-dance and forgetting all about Owen. At last they collapsed into a heap on the Bottom, and lay gasping and bubbling until their trance condition wore off. Then they remembered Owen. Sedilla looked at him quizzically.

"Are you moulting that old skin?" she asked slowly; then added kindly, thinking she might have offended him, "Such a trying time, moulting, so difficult to look one's best."

"Yes," agreed Daphnia. "You do seem to be having particular difficulty. Do all Homo Sapiens have to go through that? Your feet look rather ... well, comic, I'm afraid."

"No, not exactly," said Owen, looking down rather sheepishly at his wet shoes and the soggy socks wrinkled around his ankles. "I just ... well, it's just temporary."

"But you will have finished your moult in time for my wedding, won't you?"

"Yes, of course, Faluffel. I'll be taking them off, later."

'Later' ... Owen suddenly realised he'd been answering all their questions and asking none himself. He must learn something about his surroundings. What should he do to be safe? What would happen at night? He was about to begin, when a huge dark yellow shape loomed up quite close. The water-fleas shrieked, then quickly swam away. "But you are my friends?" shouted Owen after the retreating forms. "You will be my friends won't you?"

"Yes, yes, we will be your friends, of course we will; but mind the Salamander – beware the Salamander," came their reply in ripples from where they had disappeared. But their words were all distorted in ripples, and their warning was lost ... And it came far too late.

*It was the same newt he'd seen that day
so innocently sunning itself on the small stone ...
only now it was as terrifyingly large as Owen was helplessly tiny.*

4

THE SALAMANDER

The reptile had seen him. It was vast; as big as a dinosaur and very like one. Perhaps it was a dinosaur! The body was long, the skin rough and horny like a crocodile's, but with horrible warts and wrinkled pores all over it. Arched high over the head and running down the full length of the neck was a great serrated crest which waved to and fro in the water. The creature's underbelly was the brightest yellowy-orange that Owen had ever seen, and covered with large black spots like some awful disease. Owen tried to run away but his feet had gone completely stiff and wouldn't move. He cowered, unable to hide or defend himself. So this was the reason for the water-fleas turning and pausing as they danced along: it was to look out for the enemy, who might come at them suddenly from any angle they weren't expecting.

As the huge face bent down to scrutinise him, Owen staggered back with a cry. The giant eye had in it a look of absolute hatred, and he recognised the monster. It was the same newt he'd seen that day so innocently sunning itself on the small stone ... only now it was as terrifyingly large as Owen was helplessly tiny.

"Yes, it's you, isn't it? And I, the great crested newt, Triturus Cristatus, have been watching you for some time, just to make sure it WAS you," the voice bellowed. "You, who disturbed my rest and scared the wits out of me with your huge goggling eyes. Well, where are they NOW? Ahha! So they were a sham, were they? Well, I'm not frightened of you now. In fact I may well EAT you."

With these words, the reptile thrust out one of its ghastly webbed feet and covered Owen's foot so that he couldn't escape. For a fleeting moment Owen wished he still had his pebbly glasses so that he could frighten the monster. He put his hand into his pocket, searching for something he could use as a weapon, not daring to look away from the huge eye so full of hate. All his hand met was a large paper-clip ... but then there was a swish of water and a yawning chasm opened in front of him. He felt himself being sucked into the darkness on a huge pink tongue, upon which he stuck like a fly on a fly-paper. There was a smack and the colossal jaws clamped shut behind him, leaving him in total darkness.

Desperately he fought his way along the tongue and managed to hang onto the edge of a giant row of tooth-like bumps. By wedging his elbow between two of these, he was able to bend open one end of the paper-clip. Already he could feel a great upheaval, obviously the beginning of a swallowing motion. The tongue curled backwards, pushing him over and loosening his grip on the teeth. Preferring the tongue to the possibility of being crushed by the teeth, he let go and, holding the paper-clip with both hands at arm's length, was swallowed.

Owen managed to push the end of the paper-clip into the fleshy wall of the throat as it rushed past him, but the force of the swallow, dragged him on. Darkness and suffocation were beginning to overcome him but he could hear the gurgling sounds of the stomach that awaited him. Then suddenly the swallow was brought to a halt. To his surprise, he started to travel even faster in the opposite direction. There was a whooshing noise and, still holding tightly onto the paper-clip, Owen was ejected from the mouth of the Salamander and sent hurtling through the water. He landed in the mud.

"Salamanders," roared an angry voice, "find little boys disagreeable. They tickle the throat."

The roaring sound-waves and a storm of sediment engulfed Owen as the gigantic beast shuffled off into the distance, leaving him stupefied on the silt.

"You nearly had it there," said another huge but sluggish voice next to him. Owen was still shaken and dazed but he raised his head and saw, to his dismay, that another dinosaur creature was appearing through the settling mud. It had a vast crinkled head with two terrifying horns. The eyes, situated at the base of each tentacle-horn, gazed down at him from a great height.

Owen shuddered and backed away from the stern unblinking stare. "Something else that wants to eat me I suppose," he muttered to himself, wishing he was at home.

"Don't worry," said the monster in a reassuring tone, "I'm certainly not going to eat you. Anyway, I'm strictly vegetarian," he added in his slow drawling voice. "I only eat algae and plant-forms which I rasp with my radula ... my moveable band of teeth."

"Oh I see," said Owen, feeling very relieved, "and who are you please, Sir? I'm Homo Sapiens – a small one. You remind me of a dinosaur."

"I'm the Great Pond Snail, Limnea Stagnalis, little one ... a gastropod, and from an ancient line."

"So you are," said Owen. He was very pleased. He liked snails: they were slow like himself. It was strange to see a snail so large. But knowing the creature was not a dinosaur made the menacing horns and wrinkled face seem much kindlier. Behind the horns, the frilly snail-body disappeard into what looked at first like an immense cave but which, on closer inspection, was a perfect conical shell with intricate brown markings.

"And if I were you," continued the snail in his heavy voice, "I should be seeking some shelter before nightfall. On the Bottom it gets dark very early. I suppose," he pointed to a shiny surface in the distance, "that is your house? It certainly fell in with you; in fact it almost did for me. If I were you I'd hide in it quickly, before someone else bags it. Houses are very scarce down here nowadays. I, of course, have no need of one myself ... my shell, don't you know..."

"But will Sedilla be able to find me when she calls for me to go to the wedding tomorrow?" Owen asked. "I'd hate her not to find me."

"Sedilla? Oh yes, I know Sedilla. I'll tell her. I'm sliding towards the Centre of the Pond early tomorrow morning. Don't you worry."

Owen began to thank him for all his kindness and advice but then he saw the snail wasn't listening. He had yawned and withdrawn into his shell for the night.

The Pond was growing dark. A murkiness penetrated to mud-level, dimming the light between the rocks and reeds and deepening the shadows. Now the snail had withdrawn, Owen was scared. The memory of his recent escape from an unsavoury death filled him with anxiety. He looked across at the shiny surface the snail had pointed to, and made his way towards it.

As he drew nearer, the reeds thickened and turned into a forest whose trunks, unlike the forests above, were bulbous and green. Instead of branches, heavily-fronded stems turned and twisted sluggishly in the slow current which barely moved along the bottom. Owen wound his way through the reeds, bending the branches aside until eventually the enormous shiny thing came into view. Its smooth exterior reflected the last rays of light that slanted down through the water. Then as Owen came up to the walls of the house, he stopped short. Someone had indeed bagged it first. There, lying in wait for him, was a huge green giant, well-camouflaged, lying stock still on his side. He was staring straight at Owen. Owen dared not go a step further. Then, through his fear, something odd struck him. It was a human figure, wearing a human costume. How puzzling. Then all at once, laughing at his stupidity, he ran towards the printed 'Green Giant' label stuck onto his own jam-jar. It had landed on its side and was almost entirely covered by the waving reed-forest, which is why Owen hadn't recognised its shape from afar.

So that's what the snail meant when he said 'it' had fallen in with me. The jar is so large, it will make a wonderful place to stay ... a palace even ... "I name you Jam-Jar Palace," he announced as he entered his glass home.

The jar had obviously been heavy enough to bury itself partially in the mud when it reached the Bottom, for a flat layer of sediment had formed a floor inside, ideal for lying on. Through the glass walls, Owen would be able to identify as friend or enemy anyone who approached. As an extra precaution, he decided to seal the entrance against all possible invaders by bending some of the weed-branches over and into the rim. Even though they were flexible and light, it took all his strength to bend them. He had to build up a network of branches lower down and climb on this in order to reach the higher branches. It was pitch dark by the time he had finished. Tired but satisfied, he lay down and fell fast asleep.

When Owen awoke, the sun was already bathing the walls of Jam-Jar Palace in its warm yellowy-green light. I'm in a jam-jar at the bottom of the pond, he thought. He felt strange and a long, long way from home. There he had just one small window in his room; here all around was window and outside was weird landscape. He turned over on the soft sediment and fell asleep again.

The second time Owen awoke, he absent-mindedly reached

for his glasses. He usually put these on before opening his eyes, as they were his eyes to him. When he found they were now gone and realised again where he was, he was happier than he'd ever been. This was much better than being at home. Usually he worried about school when he awoke. Now there was no school. He got up. There was no bed to make, and as for washing, he was completely surrounded by water. Was he clean though? He walked over and inspected his reflection in the glass wall. He was clean all over. He would never have to wash again! Then something occurred to him. Why not go a step further and not even bother about dressing and undressing; tying shoe-laces, doing up zips and buttons, pulling up socks? His mother had told him never to wear wet things, yet here he was, not only wearing sopping wet pullover and shorts, but having slept in them as well. He recalled what Daphnia had remarked about his wrinkled socks and sneakers. He sat down and took off his shoes. This was difficult. The laces were soggy and had shrunk into knots. He remembered the opened paper-clip in his pocket and used this to ease the knots open. He took off his socks and stuffed them inside the shoes.

Then he decided to see what else he had on him. He emptied the pockets of his shorts – there was a handkerchief which had turned into a nasty wet rag, two toffees in cellophane wrappers, his lucky 5p piece, a small length of string, a pencil which had floated up to the ceiling of the jar, his empty glasses–case. Even his mobile phone, which he found in his other pocket, had shrunk down with him. "I wonder if I can get hold of Bethan and tell her where I am?" He dialled her number. Somebody answered it and he spoke as loudly as he could into it.

"Who's that speaking? Who's that squeaking? I can't hear you. I can't hear you. Speak up! Speak up! Is that you, Owen, trying to be funny? Silly Owen! I can't hear you." It was Bethan, and she had turned him off as hopeless. "I know, I'll text her," Owen thought.

"B help Im blow grn pnd..." but even as he was doing so, some bubbles started to squeeze their way out of the mobile and the text message faded away and the phone no longer worked.

"I don't really blame it. It's been under water all night." He flung the useless thing down and with it, any ideas of contact with the old, difficult world above he'd left behind. Instead, he put the rest of his possessions from above into his glasses-case – including the paper-clip, which he bent back into shape and put this into his pocket. Now he was ready for the day. It was a very special day: Faluffel's wedding day. Did he look his best? Again he studied his reflection and was happy with it. The goggle-eyed 'thing' with its short-sighted worried look, greasy hair and pale complexion had disappeared. Now his face looked as he had always wanted it to look. His hair wafted and waved around his head, sometimes into curls, sometimes into long, reed-like tapers. It was a constantly-changing style which pleased him. Now that his socks, shoes and glasses were gone he felt free. He loved the feel of soft water running between his toes. Now he would be able to tell Sedilla, Daphnia and Faluffel that he had finished his 'moult' in time for the wedding – and pretend that this was what he usually looked like.

He sat on a large rock and started to eat a toffee,
rolling it round his mouth, trying to make it last
as long as he could. It tasted delicious.

5

PONDERING

Parting two of the giant leaf-fronds, Owen slipped out through the door-covering. Above the Pond, he had always been so worried about tripping, or dropping things, that he had missed what was going on around him. Today would be a day of discovery. He would not need to day-dream. He felt more lively and awake than he ever did at breakfast-time at home.

Breakfast! He suddenly realised he was hungry. He only possessed two toffees and after that what was there for boys to eat at the bottom of a pond? He didn't know. Perhaps Sedilla would tell him. He decided to stay near Jam-Jar Palace and ask her when she came along. He sat on a large rock and started to eat a toffee, rolling it round his mouth, trying to make it last as long as he could. It tasted delicious.

"That thing you're sucking smells horribly sweet to me." Sedilla complained, appearing from behind the reeds. Owen jumped.

"Oh, Sedilla, thank goodness it's you. I was concentrating so hard on my toffee I forgot about everything else."

"Ah, that's pondering. You'll soon get used to it; just enjoying things as they happen, one at a time. You find out so much that way; appreciate things far more."

"Yes, I'm beginning to discover that already with this sweet."

"No, not 'discover,'" corrected Sedilla. "Discovering is a different thing altogether. Pondering is inactive. It goes on inside your head. It's a kind of peaceful thinking all Pond creatures do. Discovery, on the other hand, involves rushing about, meeting people, and observing new things. We in Ponds love discovery. You can of course ponder about your discoveries just as you can discover things to ponder, but you must never confuse one with the other … anyway," she said, seeing that Owen did look confused, "what is that horrid sweet-thing you're eating? It smells disgusting."

Owen smiled. He realised that 'thing' in Pond speech was a derogatory word and not merely a word for something you didn't know the name of. "The thing I'm sucking," he answered, "is a toffee from above the Green. I'm hungry and I don't know what boys are meant to eat down here. I hoped you might know because I only have one toffee left and that's dissolving fast."

"Well, I shouldn't eat that if I were you. There are a lot of juicy things to nibble once you have tried out what you can eat and what you can't. You need only learn to spit it out if it doesn't agree."

"But we were never allowed to spit things out if they didn't agree, above the Green," said Owen, shocked. "In fact, we were often made to eat things even if they didn't agree with us at all." He thought about school sausages and 'stodge'.

"Sounds perfectly horrid above the Green to me," said Sedilla.

"Yes, you may be right," Owen reflected. "I hated old bread-and-butter pudding and warmed up bubble-and-squeak, but I had to eat them just the same."

Sedilla laughed in a series of ripples at the idea of eating bubbles; and weren't squeaks the noises that most Pond people made?"

"Well, you need eat no 'old' food down here. Below the Green most things are fresh and nourishing. Even the water you breathe is filled with goodness, which is probably why you haven't been hungry before. Down here we don't eat from necessity, as you seem to do above the Green. We eat for pure pleasure. Normally we eat as we go along, but sometimes we arrange special feasts if there's an important occasion to celebrate, as there is today. Faluffel's wedding feast is this afternoon. Oh dear," Sedilla suddenly sighed, "that's if it all goes smoothly." And she sat down on the bottom and hid her face in her feathery hands.

"What's the matter?" asked Owen. He hadn't seen Sedilla look sad before and it quite upset him. Sadness didn't suit a water-flea; they were so bouncy. And Sedilla was the nicest creature he had ever met. He ran over to her and put his arm around her shiny shell. "Please, tell me what could go wrong. I'll help if I can."

"That's very sweet of you," said Sedilla, smiling once more, "but it really is very worrying. Sit down. I'll have to tell you sooner or later, so it might as well be now."

Owen settled on the rock while Sedilla told him the story.

"You see, Faluffel, my youngest sister, fell deeply in love with one of the most agreeable creatures in the whole Pond, Charles Copepod. He is head of the Copepods. The Copepods are strange. There are as many of them in the Pond as there are water-fleas. They tend to compete with us socially and often resent us. But Charles is different. He's strong and handsome, kind and terribly polite. They fell in love at first sight and, after many difficulties, are to be married today."

"But won't that unite the water-fleas and Copepods?" asked Owen.

"Yes, that's what should have happened; but you see Charles has a sister called Cyclops Copepod and she's really horrid. She has one large red eye glowing in the middle of her forehead. She's brash and fierce, rude and cruel. She doesn't want to lose her brother Charles because he is all she's got. The rest of the immediate family was eaten long ago."

"Oh, how awful for them," said Owen, horrified, not knowing quite what to say.

"Yes, it was awful," said Sedilla, "but the last words their mother said to Charles, as she disappeared into a Stickleback's mouth, were, 'Take care of your sister Cyclops!' So you see Charles, who is very kind, felt obliged to do so. Nobody else wants anything to do with Cyclops. She never helps anyone in the Pond. Poor Charles is always having to make allowances for her. Well, anyway, Faluffel fell in love with Charles, and she *is* very beautiful, don't you think?"

"Yes, very," Owen agreed.

"You can imagine why Cyclops grew jealous. She's done all she can to prevent the marriage. She's even turned some of the Copepods against Charles. So today, you see, when Charles has at last insisted that he and Faluffel marry, we've somehow to calm the waters and see that everything runs smoothly."

"Oh, I do hope it does," said Owen, "and I'll help if I can."

"You are kind. I feel quite recovered," said Sedilla, stroking his head. She wondered whether this boy-creature from above the Green might have some special wisdom that could help. Aloud she said, "But it's all been so very difficult. Cyclops' followers have formed themselves into a powerful gang. Even on my way here some nasty creatures warned me against the marriage, saying it would upset the equilibrium of the Pond. Oh, shhh! Here come Daphnia and Faluffel … not a word about what we've been saying. I don't want to upset Faluffel on her wedding day. Quick, talk about something else."

"And what will we be eating at the feast?" Owen asked quickly.

"Marvellous food of every kind," said Faluffel, hopping up.

"Which is why we're late," explained Daphnia, flopping down onto the silt. "We've done so much Algae-gathering we're quite exhausted."

"What is Algae?" asked Owen.

"My, you are ignorant," Daphnia gasped. "Fancy not knowing about Algae. You say you are a wise boy-Homo Sapiens, but you don't seem to be clever at all."

"Oh, but I'm only at the boy ... I mean larval stage, the learning stage," said Owen quickly. "We get wiser as we grow up."

"But the Algae are the most important part of our Pond. They cover nearly the whole surface. Whatever could you have thought the Green was?"

"Is the Green all Algae then?" Owen asked.

"Yes, of course it is, silly – that and Duck-weed makes the Green." Faluffel collapsed with laughter next to Daphnia.

"They give us food and oxygen to breathe," explained Sedilla, "and all by using the light from our Sun. The process is called photosynthesis."

"Whatever does *that* mean?" asked Owen, feeling even smaller.

"Really, your ignorance astounds me," said Sedilla. "Have you *no* knowledge of the Greek?"

"No," said Owen, his eyes widening. These Pond-creatures were putting him to shame. "Please explain."

"It's a very simple Greek word. *Photo* means light, and *synthesis* means putting-together. So Photosynthesis means light-putting-together. That wasn't too difficult, was it?"

"No, not at all," said Owen, "and I'm glad to be learning some Greek."

"Well, listen carefully," Sedilla continued. "With the help of their chlorophyll, which is the greenness we see in the Algae and Duck-weed, they're able to take in and store light from the Sun. Then with carbon dioxide which they extract from the air or water, they make sugars. It's these sugars that make the Green taste absolutely delicious; and as a waste-product, they give out oxygen for us to breathe through our skins. You'll understand it all much better when we go up to the Green."

Owen pondered a while, entranced. So that was why he hadn't drowned. He was breathing through his entire skin. How clever! And how nice it would be to go up and see the Green and taste it too. Then his face fell. "Did you say go up to the Green?"

"Yes, Up is where the Green is, isn't it? You ought to know, you fell in through it in the first place."

"Yes, I know I did, but that was because I was coming down, not going up. I'm afraid I don't know how to go up."

"Don't know how to go up?" repeated Sedilla incredulously. "But surely you can swim?"

Owen hung his head. That was what they had tried to make him do at the seaside. The salt got into his eyes and nose and he'd been frightened of drowning. Although he was under water here and had not drowned, the fact remained, he simply couldn't swim.

Faluffel looked crestfallen.

"But you won't be able to come to my wedding ceremony. All Pond-creatures get married at the Green. We can't possibly be married anywhere else."

"He'll still be able to come to the feast, though," said Daphnia, comfortingly. "That's at the Stone Table on the Bottom. But it's sad all the same ..."

"I like you better now that your legs have finished moulting and you're finally out of your old skin," ventured Faluffel gently, in an effort to cheer him up and change the subject.

"We did think you looked rather thing-like in your unfinished moult," said Sedilla.

Owen felt happier. He told them all about the Salamander and how he'd been spat out.

"Why didn't you swim away quickly like us?" asked Faluffel – and then her whole body turned red with embarrassment as she realised what she'd said.

"Shush, Faluffel," cried Sedilla angrily. "Now look what you've done. You've reminded him all over again."

"Poor Owen," said Daphnia, "but Faluffel's right, really. We can't escape from the fact that you're unable to swim, so I'll teach you. What's the use of walking along the Bottom all your life? It's dark and the Sun doesn't shine so strongly here. Besides, you do want to meet more Pond-creatures, don't you?"

"Yes, of course. I want to meet everybody."

This last remark was met by titters from all three fleas, who wriggled their feet and squiggled their arms with glee, and did a little hopping dance together.

"Sadly," said Daphnia eventually, "you could never meet everybody. We only know a fraction of them ourselves. There are hundreds and hundreds of creatures who we'll never meet. The Pond is vastly over-crowded and most creatures are larger than we are. That's why you should learn to swim away from danger – and you must certainly never go near the Edge."

"The Edge? Do you mean the Edge of the Pond?"

"Yes, of course she does, silly," said Faluffel. "What else has an Edge except the Pond? I've heard tell that the Edge goes all the way round it. I've never been near it and wouldn't want to; but I know there are dark holes where Furry Monsters live."

"And they're not at all nice to know," Daphnia continued. "The Water-vole has quivering whiskers and ghastly teeth and the Water-shrew has cruel claws and a pointed snout. We don't like any of them."

"Then I don't want to meet any Furry Monsters, thank you," said Owen. "I'd like to meet more Squiggly-wigglies like you. I know all about Squiggly-wigglies."

"What do you know about us?" giggled Daphnia.

"And even before you fell in?" squeaked Faluffel.

"Yes," said Owen proudly. "We learned all about you from the whiteboard ..." He was just about to add "and saw you through the microscope" when he realised that would be tactless. Stealing Squiggly-wigglies from the Pond and putting them in cold glass slides was like committing murder. He must *never* mention that; so instead, he said "... and we learnt your classification from Mr Allbright, the Natural History master. That's why I could place Sedilla as a water-flea, the moment I saw her."

"Well, I'm very flattered that you know all about me and not the Furry Monsters," said Sedilla.

"Yes, but that's my fault really. You see, I've never seen a Furry Monster. I was always too slow because of my short-sightedness."

"No, not short-sightedness. Down here being short-sighted means you've overlooked something, and that is most unwise. It could lead to a very bad accident indeed. For example, you're probably not even aware that the 'rock' you're sitting on is poor old Lamellibranch, the fresh-water mussel."

"Oh! Said Owen, jumping up in confusion. "I'm so sorry."

"Sit down. Sit down. He doesn't mind at all. He's a very old bivalve who doesn't move around much. He's already half buried in the Bottom, which is probably why you didn't see what he was. He usually likes to keep very still, poor dear." Sedilla bent forward and whispered in Owen's ear: "He's only got one muscular foot to propel himself along with anyway, so when he does move about, it's very slow indeed." Then she continued loudly, "But you love to hear all the Pond-chatter, don't you, Mollusc dear?" and she patted his shell affectionately.

In answer, Owen felt the rock beneath him shift slightly. There was a strange gurgle and a small, flattened bubble squeezed out between the upper and lower shell, releasing itself into the water. Then the shell clammed tightly shut and the Mollusc settled down again.

"Now, where were we? Oh yes, so keep to the Centre of the Pond and you'll be safe. The Furry Monsters live near the Edge where they have their holes. They love the dark, and hardly ever go to the Centre. Everything happens there; all big social events and wedding feasts," she smiled, turning to Faluffel.

"Oh, so that's why the Centre must be the busiest part of the Pond."

"Of course. Everyone wants to live there. Who could possibly want to live near the Edge, with the Monsters around? *You* live far too near the Edge for comfort, and although you didn't know, it was a little risky for us to come and collect you. We just had to come and inspect your huge shiny house when it fell in with such a Big Splash yesterday, though. We couldn't resist it. It's not often that such large real estate falls in."

"Thank you. I do appreciate it. I've no other friends except for the Great Pond Snail ... and the Mollusc, of course," he added quickly as the rock below him began to shift. "And as for living here, I couldn't help it. This is the place where my Jar decided to fall in, but I'd love to go to the Centre."

"You shall. Right away. In fact," she continued, putting her fluffy arm around Owen's shoulder, "the Centre also happens to be where the Hornwort forest grows, and as the Hornworts have such suitable leaves from which to launch yourself, that's where the newly-hatched creatures practise their swimming if they're having difficulties."

Owen realised that going to the Centre would mean learning how to swim as well as having a wedding-feast. He resigned himself to the fact that he would make no real discoveries unless he could swim, and said he would try. They all smiled and patted him with their feathery arms.

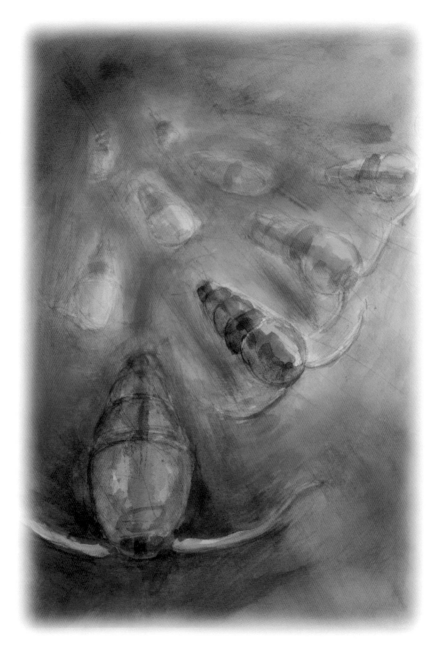

The shoal of Copepods had as much right to be there as anyone else,
yet the way they were swimming – all together in a pack
– was more like a warning, a show of force.

6

THE AMBUSH

The journey to the Centre of the pond was full of mysteries for Owen, so you can imagine his excitement and surprise when they finally reached the City Walls and he saw that they were composed of an enormous bicycle, very rusty and with the front wheel badly buckled. Its gigantic frame stretched as far as he could see in every direction. Pond sponges had been encouraged to fill in the gaps in the rusty frame. The sponges were banked up together, smothering rocks, pebbles and bits of wood that had been wedged through various parts of the bicycle. Their furry coverings, made of minute silica-spicules, were sharp enough to discourage any unwanted creatures.

Owen was pleased to see the Great Pond Snail guarding the entrance. Limnea Stagnalis greeted them politely and wished Faluffel the best of luck as they passed through. Travelling on, they soon reached a dreamy place where cool currents filtered through the fronds and wafted round reeds. There, hidden among pebbles and mud or stuck to the Pond-weeds, were funnels, sacs, pouches, tunnels and tubes made from tiny particles of sand bound together with sticky secretions. Some were artfully constructed from pieces of reed folded and woven together; others from mud smoothed out and reinforced with little pebbles, and there were comfortable nets spun from fine strands of silk. Inside them, all sorts of larvae were hatching or undergoing metamorphosis to become something else.

"I never realised there was so much hatching out at the Bottom of Ponds," said Owen, astonished. "It's rather like a giant nursery."

"Oh yes, you have to tread very gently when you pass through the Nurseries. The larvae are sensitive to any kind of vibration. That's why they're here, away from the bustle of the Centre, yet inside the protection of the City Walls. Hatching is such a delicate operation; takes so much pondering."

They left the Nurseries, threading their way through the outskirts of the City.

Sedilla had just started to tell Owen about the Protozoa, the simple folk who lived in that area, when suddenly a purplish streak flashed past so close and low that Sedilla could see the orange and green of each creature's body-segments. She felt uneasy. The shoal of Copepods had as much right to be there as anyone else, yet the way they were swimming – all together in a pack – was more like a warning, a show of force.

"That's what it was like coming here this morning," whispered Faluffel hoarsely, "but we didn't want to tell you."

"It happened to me too," said Sedilla, growing alarmed.

"We'll just have to ignore them," said Daphnia, "they're only making a nuisance of themselves … sort of registering a complaint. They can't really harm us in the Centre; not with everyone around."

"Yes, you're right, Daphnia. There's no need to upset ourselves. We'll carry on and show we're not concerned. What was I saying? Oh yes," Sedilla continued, trying to sound cheerful, "the Protozoa. They're Plankters like us but of such a simple structure, they only have one cell. Because of their small size and simple ways of getting about, they tend to congregate here in the outskirts. They're always in a terrible hurry, especially to reproduce. They merely divide into two whenever they feel the urge. Ah, look over there! There's a Protozoan. It's Euglena, Euglena Flagellata."

Euglena, a tube-shaped creature was propelling herself along with her small flagellum, which vibrated at a terrific rate. As she passed in front of them, she changed from a tube into a pear-shape.

"Euglena has a stretchy transparent covering, you see," whispered Sedilla, "so she can change her one cell into all kinds of different shapes, just for variety. She likes to show off and we really shouldn't stare at her like this. She'll get conceited and grow too big for her membrane! Come on."

"I'd like to be able to change my shape and be different all the time," said Owen. "My mother often tries to change her shape; she's always saying 'I wish I had a bit more here and a little less there'. She wears an elastic thing too, but it doesn't seem to change her outline. In fact, it makes her more stiff and definite than she was before."

Sedilla collapsed in a fit of giggles at the idea of Owen's mother in an elastic 'thing'; but stopped short when a warning cry from Faluffel gave them only enough time to jump aside before a purple shoal streamed past again, gleaming and evil. The force of their passage through the water knocked Owen and Sedilla sideways, throwing them against the weed-trunks. Looking around, Sedilla saw they were completely alone in the glade.

"Quick! Faluffel, Owen, Daphnia, stay together. Don't let them separate Faluffel from us."

Faluffel and Daphnia were barely able to join Owen and Sedilla before the shoal, now assembled at the end of the glade, darted round and charged straight at them.

"Duck at the very last moment," ordered Sedilla. "It's our only hope."

Compact in shape, the shoal smashed straight through the middle of them and was away almost before they had ducked. But Owen grabbed angrily at the last Copepod, who was a little out of line. Finding that he was holding onto an antenna, he gave it a hard tug, toppling the creature into a somersault so that its head crashed on the ground. The Copepod shrieked, then swam off whimpering to join the rest of the shoal.

"Owen, what have you done? How stupid you are!" shouted Sedilla. Her eyes had become strained and afraid.

"But they've no right to do this to us," said Owen, colouring. "I was only trying to protect you all. What's wrong?"

"Oh, Owen, don't you see, that's exactly what they want us to do, start to fight back. Before, they were mobbing; now we haven't a chance. There'll be a real fight, and there are so many more of them. We'll have to make for cover. Look, over there in that tangle of weeds. Swim fast ..."

But they remembered just in time that Owen couldn't swim, and not wishing to leave him, started to race hard with him over the silt.

"Please swim away quickly and leave me!" Owen cried.

"No, we can't leave you. Hurry, they're coming back."

But it was useless, the shoal was upon them. They stopped and huddled closely together as the purple, orange and green mass exploded above their heads. At once the water was filled with bristling feet, scrabbling at their faces, lashing at their arms. Owen felt his hair pulled sharply and saw the water-fleas' antennae crushed together. They tried to form a circle by pressing their heads and soft underbellies inwards for protection. Then, as the shoal left to re-arrange itself for a further attack, Sedilla threw up her head and shouted:

"Help, Protozoa! Help us!"

Why was no-one else around? How stupid to let themselves be trapped in such a lonely glade.

"Help, Protozoa! Help us!" she cried again.

There was no answer. Meanwhile the water was filled with a strange humming noise; a monotonous droning on one pitch.

"The battle-call of the Copepods," warned Sedilla. "Then they're closing in for a final attack … we *must* make for the undergrowth this time."

As they dived into the tangled weeds, the shoal was all about them, slashing the water, beating the undergrowth and tearing it away in great chunks in their frenzy to find their victims. Then suddenly the water was filled with the noise of other creatures.

"Oh, thank the Sun. The Protozoa have come to our rescue." In spite of his fear, Owen was amazed at those who were helping. A strange slipper-creature was slapping the Copepods from behind. Something with an armoured shell-covering of sand, pebbles, twigs and other debris slid through the water walloping the enemy with his shell, bashing at them with his bits and pieces. A huge green 'cannon ball' whizzed through the shoal, causing disarray. A creature that Owen recognised as Amoeba was kicking out with feet formed from its jelloid body. Then he saw Euglena. Although she was attempting to fight, she succeeded only in making a nuisance of herself, constantly changing shape and generally getting in the way.

All at once there was a rumbling noise in the distance, and a huge spiky ball came hurtling by like heavy artillery.

"The Sun-animalcule Heliozoa has arrived! Jump clear!"

The hard-cased object, with long prickly extensions shooting out from its body, charged through the water, tumbling over and over as it came. The Copepods screamed and parted.

Recklessly, the huge ball rode through them, narrowly missing Faluffel and Daphnia in its progress. Soon the shoal had dispersed and fled. But Sedilla saw, to her horror, that one of the Copepods had been impaled upon a prickle and was being spun round and round as the ball rolled out of sight.

Daphnia and Faluffel were untangling themselves from the reeds. Faluffel was crying "My wedding! I'll look awful for my wedding."

"No you won't," Daphnia assured her while she straightened her feet and uncrumpled her antennae. "You're hardly scratched. Look at poor Owen who hasn't got a shell. He's scratched far worse."

Owen's back hurt quite badly. But for some reason it didn't sting as much as it might have done above the Green.

"The water will soothe away the pain, Owen, and the scratches will soon heal," Sedilla comforted him. "Come, we must all go and thank the Protozoa for saving our lives."

The Protozoa were resting … except for the Sun-animalcule Heliozoa who was nowhere to be seen. Sedilla thought he had wisely gone into hiding after realising he had killed a Copepod.

"There will be reprisals and more trouble," she whispered fearfully, but aloud she thanked the Protozoa warmly for their help and asked them to convey her thanks to Heliozoa as well.

"Yes, of course," promised Difflugia, who was in command, "and we've decided to accompany you to the Centre, to make sure you're quite safe."

They all make their way to the Centre. Volvox the green 'cannon ball' bounced along beside Sedilla, the jelloid Amoeba, and elasticated Euglena accompanied Faluffel, and the Slipper-animalcule (who was shaped exactly like a fluffy bedroom-slipper) trod water delicately above Daphnia's head. Difflugia the armoured animalcule wobbled along next to Owen.

"How did you get such a super shell?" he asked her.

"It was very easy really," she said, and her voice under its shell sounded muffled, as if she was speaking from under an upturned basin. "First I secreted a sticky layer over myself; then I selected all sorts of foreign matter, laid them in a design, and simply rolled over them till they stuck."

"I'd love to have a house like yours. I'd stick onto it things like my bicycle wheel, and bits of old car, and flower-pots and logs." Owen visualised his house as they walked along. It would be wonderful. The best house in the world.

They were climbing the uphill slope that lead to the Centre. Ahead, the Pond-light grew brighter, covering the dense vegetation with a green radiance. Behind him, Owen heard Volvox grumble, then stop.

"Poor thing, the light is beginning to stimulate him into photosynthesising. We must take him back into the dark before he starts turning into a plant," advised Difflugia. "He's so very nearly a plant and not an animal. The borderline is extremely close with us Protozoa you understand."

"Poor Volvox, he does look a little green. You must go at once," said Sedilla. "And thank you all very much."

"Goodbye," they chorused, and swam off, helping Volvox to bounce along.

"Please, what is an animalcule?" asked Owen, his curiosity getting the better of him.

"Animalcule just means a microscopic animal, like us."

"Does that mean I'm an animalcule too? A boy-animalcule?"

"Yes, I suppose so. It sounds rather nice, boy-animalcule. You can be called that if you like from now on. I'll include it in your formal introductions."

"Oh please do," said Owen, jumping with delight, and he ran up the rest of the slope shouting "Boy-animalcule, boy-animalcule!" at the top of his voice.

*Many of the smaller creatures had actually got into bubbles
and were travelling upwards smiling and waving from inside.*

7

THE CENTRE

At the top of the ridge, Owen came to a halt and gasped in amazement at the sight spread out before him. The brown mud they had been walking on for so long came to an abrupt end in the hollow of a basin-shaped valley. In its place was a thick layer of mossy sphagnum with long strands of iridescent Algae sparkling in silver and green. The submerged vegetation was like a drowned meadow, or an immense carpet, from which rose the Hornworts. Their roots trailed above the ground, and from their branches sprang a mass of small shiny pointed leaves which radiated from each stem and formed little leafy platforms. Fronds of Milfoil weed waved back and forth, and the whole scene was bathed in a beautiful light as the Sun shone greenly from above.

Wherever the shafts of light touched the moss, streaks of silver bubbles welled up from its depths. Pond-creatures of all shapes and sizes were bouncing on the springy carpet or playing with bubbles. Larger creatures were being carried to the surface clinging to the outside of the bubbles. There they would let go, crying "Wheeeeee" all the way down to the moss, which bounced them up to fall and bounce again. Many of the smaller creatures had actually got into bubbles and were travelling upwards smiling and waving from inside. Some early Hatchers were practicing their swimming, launching themselves from the leafy platforms, and adults stood nearby instructing them. Others milled around discussing news with friends. There was a great deal of laughter and activity.

"How wonderful," said Owen. "Everyone seems to be having such a good time. Playing with bubbles looks great fun."

"Of course it's fun. Most things are fun. That's what we are here for, isn't it?" Sedilla turned and looked at Owen quizzically. "What do you think life is for?"

Owen had never really thought about this. As far as he was concerned, life went on day after day but what it was for was a big question.

"I suppose we're taught that living properly is giving things up for others, thinking of them before ourselves, not being greedy or selfish, or impatient ..."

"That sounds awfully boring," Sedilla commented. "The whole point of living is to enjoy yourself as much as possible."

Again Owen was shocked. That wasn't what he'd been taught above the Green. It would take a lot of pondering.

"It doesn't mean that you cannot be useful, of course. Being useful makes you feel good and gives you a happy feeling inside. I even enjoy knowing that I'll be useful when I die."

"How?" he asked.

"Well, when you die, you sink to the Bottom, even if you're eaten by another creature first. There with the remains of other plants and animals, you form the mud or Detritus, which feeds the sphagnum moss. That's where you're being useful. The sphagnum ferments in the Sun-light to form our bubbles. How rewarding it must be to create such a soft landing for all the dear creatures who are falling and for those young Hatchers as they practice their swimming. Come on," Sedilla smiled, seeing that Owen was pondering hard. "We'll teach you to swim."

They walked down to join the other Pond creatures. Some were drifting along eating the Algae. Others performed in shoals, with each individual copying exactly the motion and direction of the one in front, so that the whole shoal behaved as one huge twisting wave; turning, darting, and stalling in a series of beautiful patterns.

A colony of fresh-water Shrimps swam past, crowding out the other creatures. At first Owen thought they required more space to swim because of their size, but on closer inspection he saw that the others were making way for them. Then, to his surprise, the shoal stopped short, changed direction and swam towards them. From the centre of the shoal, the biggest and oldest-looking Shrimp approached Daphnia, Faluffel and Sedilla. He looked rather like a walrus. Distinguished lines wrinkled his eyes and long whiskers trailed down on either side of his mouth. As he reached them, Sedilla, Faluffel and Daphnia bowed their heads respectfully.

"My dear," he addressed Faluffel in a kindly way, "my dear, I congratulate you on going ahead with the marriage. An admirable choice I'm told. I hope everything drifts along splendidly. My shoal and I will protect you from the Copepods during the ceremony."

"Oh, thank you. You are so kind," Faluffel beamed. She made a small curtsey, fluttering her eyes. Then the Shrimp swam away to join his shoal.

"What an honour for you," said Sedilla, filled with awe.

"I feel so proud and so relieved," said Daphnia, hugging Faluffel.

"Who are those Shrimp-people, Sedilla?" asked Owen. "Please tell me about them."

"They're a very old, respected colony whose race or genera go back a long way. So far in fact that their leader, the one who spoke, is reputed to be a relic from the Ice Age. His species was trapped in the Fresh water after the Ice Age was over. He calls himself Mysis Relicta."

"Oh, I didn't know some creatures were more important than others."

"Naturally," said Daphnia. "It depends on your history, structure and size of course. But Pond-people who try to make themselves important through sheer size are frowned upon. We are only Plankters and don't count for much; but there again, we are crustaceans like the Shrimps and not like the worms wriggling about without any crust at all."

"We shed our skins if we want to get bigger," Faluffel explained. "It's nice to have a new skin every so often, don't you agree?"

"Yes, it is," Owen had to say, remembering how he had shed his socks and shoes. He knew he had a good 'structure' inside him. He had seen the skeleton in the school cupboard. But he didn't want to boast of being from a Higher Order, so he said nothing more.

"Come on," he heard Daphnia say in a voice that implied she had taken command. "Up we go."

And to his dismay, Owen found they had stopped under a Hornwort tree a little way from where the small Hatchers were practicing. He watched them climb laboriously up the Hornwort roots onto the leafy platforms, run to the end and jump off. They made violent swimming motions with their legs through the water. But the legs went at different speeds and in different directions, causing them to sprawl on the moss. Then as the instructors shouted "No co-ordination. No co-ordination at all," the Hatchers would giggle, untangle their feet and try again.

"Oh dear, learning to swim looks very difficult," sighed Owen unhappily.

"Idiot!" Faluffel teased. "The Hatchers only find it difficult because they have so many legs. Once they learn to row them in time they can manage. But you've only got two feet! Well, four altogether," she added, looking at his arms.

"Now, off you go," coaxed Daphnia, "and remember, forwards and down."

Owen ran to the end of the leafy platform and jumped off. He put his arms in the right position but shut his eyes tight. He landed in rather a wriggly heap.

"No. No. You must dive downwards, not upwards, or you'll just go into a fall. Dive down through the water, piercing it with your hands and throwing it back behind you. Move your legs up and down in a kicking motion and *keep your eyes open*. Try again."

Owen did. Again and again. Then suddenly he understood. Swimming was entirely different from walking. In walking, the feet were the main thing. You put them out in front, and your arms and body just followed. In swimming, your head and arms led the way. It was more satisfying than walking.

Eventually, when he had learnt basic swimming, Daphnia taught him to glide. This meant that after a good push backwards with his hands, he could keep his arms pressed tightly to his sides with just his legs doing their scissor-like action. It felt wonderful.

"Good," said Daphnia. "Now we'll swim off and find poor Bosmina. She's been doing all the work arranging the feast. It's nearly noon and high time we were going up for the ceremony."

At first Owen banged into a lot of plants and sometimes other creatures, and had to apologise. Daphnia taught him to change direction by using his feet as a rudder, and he discovered that by altering the position of his toes very slightly he could twist and turn out of the Pond-people's way.

Emergency stops were more difficult. He had to bring his knees up sharply in front of his chest and press backwards with his head. At first Owen kept going into a somersault, but before long he could do emergency stops even when swimming fast.

"I think I'm beginning to enjoy swimming," he announced. This new sense of achievement suddenly made him feel very grown up.

"Good!" said Daphnia. "Very soon you'll find that swimming requires much less work. The best and fastest swimmers use so little effort they no longer have to ponder it; it all becomes second nature."

While searching for Bosmina, they waved to their friends. Everyone they met wished Faluffel well, and she grew very nervous and excited.

Sedilla was pleased by Owen's eagerness to improve himself. He was so unlike many of her friends, who had sluggish dispositions and just crawled about the Bottom all day. Now he could swim, she could accept him as a fellow Pond-creature and forget he came from above the Green.

"There's Bosmina. We've got to catch her," shrieked the water-fleas, and instantly they disappeared, leaving nothing but zig-zag lines through the water. Owen was amused at the way Pond-creatures left without warning, or when they arrived, joined in your conversation in mid-sentence, as if they'd been with you for the last half an hour. He waited on a weed-branch until they returned.

"Owen, this is Bosmina, our other water-flea cousin. Bosmina, this is Boy-animalcule Owen, who has just learned to swim."

"Charmed to meet you. I'm Bosmina Longirostris. So pleased to know you."

Bosmina was sweet. She had a body like a peanut. Her face ended in a kind of long snout, like a beak. Her bright sparkling eyes were set at the top of her face and twinkled when she spoke in her high tremolo voice. She rushed and rippled all her words together as though she had a lot to say and too little time to say it. Her peanut body hopped up and down in front of Owen, vibrating her with eager energy. He was amazed at the way she wiggled about when she was really trying to keep still.

"I'm glad you've learnt to swim," Bosmina congratulated him, "because you'll have to swim as fast as you can straight to the nearest bubbles. We're all very late. The others have been up there for ages. We'll have to go up by bubble."

"Terrific!" said Owen. "I've been longing to go inside a bubble."

As they raced along, Bosmina took Sedilla aside.

"I have to tell you something about Cyclops that you ought to know. Apparently she's still not resigned to the wedding. It took all Charles's persuasion to get her to be a Maid of Honour. She's waiting for you and Faluffel now by the White Crowfoot flowers, but they say her eye glowers with such malevolence that the petals are growing pink around her."

Sedilla sighed. What a problem it all was. But her sighs were lost in shrieks of laughter that announced their approach to the bubbles, and seeing the fun, she couldn't help feeling better. Some creatures who were falling had landed on bubbles by mistake, and had started to ascend against their will. Others were hanging on to the bubbles, first holding them back, then letting go, so they shot up out of line.

Before you could say 'mud', Bosmina, in her energetic way, grabbed Faluffel and announced shrilly: "We're going on ahead to get ready." With that they dived into the very next bubble and waved excitedly as it wobbled unsteadily upwards. As they disappeared towards the Green, Owen went back to look for Daphnia. He soon spotted her. She was swimming along rather like an old bed-spring, heaving her body through the water with a great effort.

"Poor Daphnia. We've exhausted her with your lessons," said Sedilla, "but really she shouldn't be so fat. She eats too much."

"Don't wait for me," said Daphnia. "I'll come on up when I've had a little rest."

"All right, we'll go on and meet you up there."

Sedilla led Owen to where the bubbles were forming out of the moss. He watched intently. Their emergence was a kind of squeezing out and bulging upwards process.

"Now," said Sedilla, "you must be sure to dive into the bubble at the same time as I do. Point both hands together and pierce the bubble-wall, pushing it back behind you. If you do this fast enough, the bubble will engulf you."

They chose a bubble that looked big enough for two, dived in together and sat laughing with satisfaction as a bubble-floor formed beneath them and lifted them up with a jolt. There was a whooshing sound. They were water-borne.

"How wonderful," sighed Owen, as the world beyond the bubble-skin slid past, strangely detached and smaller than them. "How nice to have one's own private bubble-craft."

There was no need to steer: the bubble already knew where it was going ... to the top.

"Oh, I do feel light-headed," said Owen suddenly. "What's happening?"

"It's all right," Sedilla giggled. "That's the gas in our bubble. On sunny days like today, bubbles that rise from the moss are full of oxygen. It's bound to make you feel a little dizzy, but you'll get used to it."

The oxygen made Owen feel as if he was in a dream. The giant stems of the Pondweed sliding past glowed iridescent green; the streams of rising bubbles sparkled like opals. Silken cocoons, slung from fibrous branches, flashed past reflecting the light. Cradles swinging from ropes stretched between weed-stems gleamed mysteriously. Inside them, shadows moved about, telling of occupants waiting to hatch. Others, more anxious to come out, made thumping sounds which echoed strangely through the Pond.

"It's always like this in late Spring," said Sedilla, "pods everywhere, egg-capsules in abundance – and it gets worse. You should see the pandemonium in early Summer, when all this," she said pointing to a row of dormant pods passing them by, hatches out. There's such squabbling and fighting for food. And all the childish questions: 'Why this?' and 'Why that?' – and the whole business of teaching them how to enjoy themselves begins all over again."

As they ascended, the bubble expanded and the objects outside looked nearer and bigger again. A translucent green filtered through the water. Creatures swam busily to and fro, separately or in shoals.

"This is the Pelagic zone, the most densely-populated area of the Pond. Most Plankters live up here, including me, as there's always a plentiful supply of food, oxygen and light."

Later they passed an enormous Pond-sponge, curled around a thick succulent stem. He was lumpy, green and covered with a hard spiky case of coral. A group of adolescent Ostracods swam past, angular in shape. They swam awkwardly and self-consciously, talking loudly and boasting.

"I remember going through that stage," said Sedilla. "Oh, look over at the moss-animalcules, the Polyzoa. Such sweet and gentle things. They live together, packed tightly into colonies, and bud furiously in Autumn. There's Plumatella Fungosa, Fredericella Sultana, and over there Cristatella. Magical, aren't they? Look at the way they move their slender bodies and flower-like crowns so delicately through the water. You'd never think, from her obvious breeding, that Victorella, stuck to that branch over there, was found in the Victoria Docks, London, after which she was named, would you?"

"However did you know that?" Owen asked, surprised.

"Ahh, It's all Pond history. Handed down from flea to flea. It probably comes from the insects, they are so knowledgeable."

"And what exactly are the Victoria Docks?" Owen asked, to test her.

"The Victoria Docks are just a larger Pond than ours, only saltier and darker and noisier, and I'm told the atmosphere is not exactly fresh – but there is some improvement going on."

"Wow! Very good!" said Owen, giggling, "and absolutely right."

They were approaching the surface now and looking upwards, they could see a vast blanket of green. The bubble grew excited and began to race faster and faster, so that Owen and Sedilla could no longer see out clearly. Distant noises burbled and gurgled, shapes flashed past; colours whizzed by in streaks. Suddenly the green intensified as the bubble hit the water-skin and exploded. It spilt its gas into the air above the Green, and tumbled its occupants downwards, whirling them through the water like spinning-tops.

"Wheeee," said Sedilla in ecstasy, as she allowed herself to twirl for a while. Then all at once she flung out her arms and legs, stopped, and went into a graceful dive, sliding down to where Owen was still falling.

"Stop you fool, stop!" she shrieked with laughter.

Owen obeyed, breaking his speed with a perfect emergency halt.

They alighted on the branch of a fat tubular stem to await Daphnia. Sedilla swung her legs through the water, but Owen, his head thrown back, stared in wonder at the Green.

All eyes turned towards the silken ropes. Looking shy and pretty,
Faluffel, escorted by Ostracod, had nearly reached Charles Copepod
and his best man, Rottifer the Rotifer.

8

The Wedding at the Green

Millions and millions of minute Algae were all crowded together, fighting and nudging one another in an effort to secure a place in the Sun. The green of their chlorophyll was so intense that where it met the yellow of the Sun, the two colours fused to produce a fluorescent glow. The light and warmth stimulated the Algae to photosynthesise, drinking in the solar energy and turning it into sugars in their bodies. There was a seething, and excitement, as though everything had been elevated to an uncontrollable state of activity. Owen looked at Sedilla. She, too had been affected. Her eyes gleamed with fervor and her antennae trembled.

"Sedilla, what is it, I feel different. Warm and happy all over my skin."

"Don't be alarmed. The Green affects everybody in the same way. We are at the Spiritual Centre, the holiest part of the Pond; bathing in the heat of the Sun, breathing in rich invigorating water, supercharged with oxygen from the Green. It makes you feel elated ... almost out of control. I expect you're feeling quite spiritual, aren't you?"

"Yes, I do feel very spiritual, thank you."

Everything up here at the Green was more beautiful and bewitching than he ever could have imagined. The wonder of it made his heart beat fast and his blood race. So here were the secrets of the Pond. This was why the middle of the Pond glowed, and why it heaved about, a luminous mixture of greens pulsing and throbbing in the Sun.

"Ah," Sedilla was saying, "I do so love the dear sweet drifting organisms. They're so responsive to the Sun, so teeming with life; so fat and juicy; so good to eat ..."

"But, Sedilla, how can you love them so much when you're going to eat them?" Owen was confused and a little indignant.

"Surely you love the things you eat, as well ... oh no, I forgot. You don't, do you?" She remembered the warmed-up bubbles and the squeaks. "You should always praise food before you eat it. Food so loves being praised."

Owen pondered this and then had to agree that it was true. He loved chocolate, and he remembered that after he'd eaten some, he often said, "you did taste nice." Yes, the more he thought about it the more it made sense.

"But aren't you afraid of being eaten yourself, Sedilla?"

"Afraid? Yes, of course I'm afraid, but one must put these things in proportion. It's silly to worry about being eaten. It could happen at any time, but you should accept it as an inevitable part of Pond-life. After all, you must hope that the thing that's eating you will enjoy you. You may be lucky, of course, and not be enjoyed, in which case you'll be spat out. I myself have been spat out more than once, I can tell you."

"And I have once," said Owen, thinking of Salamander.

"There you are then."

"And here I am ... wheeee coeeee," said Daphnia, spilling out from a bubble right above them. "Thank you for waiting."

"Well, off we go to the White Circles to join Faluffel and Cyclops," said Sedilla. "I'll swim ahead to check the way. And mind, Owen, don't touch the water-skin with your body. You may well stick to it and be eaten by someone before you have a chance to get off."

"You can, of course, go right through the water-skin in a bubble," Daphnia explained, as she and Owen swam on behind. "Usually the bubble breaks at the surface and spills you out, but if you're clever, you can catch one travelling up close to the stem of the Giant Burweed, which grows in the Centre. Bubbles tend to congregate round the crown of the plant before they burst. From there you can get through the surface-skin and look at things above the Green."

"I'd love to do that," said Owen. He was curious to see his own world again soon.

"And some day perhaps you shall," Daphnia promised, "but be careful to dive sharply down if the bubble bursts. There are nasty things stuck just below the surface film."

Soon, sure enough, Owen could see the 'nasty things'. They were among the green Algae, suspended from the film by their feet, endlessly wriggling. Black mosquito-wigglers; hundreds of them, squirming in a strange dance that involved bending up into a U-shape, then straightening out. They looked decidedly hungry. Owen winced at their ugliness. Then in contrast he saw beyond them, delicate pale white circles lying softly on the surface, parting the Green with their rounded petals. Their great glistening white arcs quivered lightly on the film; their edges fibrilated and their centres rocked rhythmically on long rolled stems. When the Sun filtered through the petals, lacy patterns flickered on the water, shooting rays of mother-of-pearl.

"It's here by the Water Crowfoot that the brides traditionally wait till they're called to be married," Daphnia explained.

But Owen wasn't really listening, for he'd seen Faluffel, sitting very nervously on one of the circles. She looked beautiful. She'd been decorated with little pieces of brightly-coloured moss and strands of delicate weed-frond. But next to her was someone who made Owen start. It was Cyclops. What a sinister-looking creature she was. Her clumsy segmented body ended in two stumpy antennae, and from every segment there sprouted numerous stiff bristles, bright green, orange, black and purple. These were far too flamboyant to be called attractive and far too numerous to be elegant ... although she obviously thought they were, for she made them bristle and crawl all the time. Attached to the top of her legs were two sacs that held some round eggs packed so tightly together that they looked as if they'd been cemented there.

Not nearly as pretty an arrangement as the water-fleas', Owen thought. But the thing he most disliked about her appearance was the red eye set right in the middle of her forehead. It glowed angrily at them as they approached.

Owen was presented to Cyclops who answered with a curt nod of her head, enquiring in a rasping, tuneless voice:

"How d'ye do? So you're the honoured guest, are you?"

The 'honoured' was emphasised in a scornful tone. Owen was taken aback. He didn't like Cyclops at all so far and it was quite obvious that she she didn't intend him to like her. Luckily, any conversation with her was prevented by the prompt arrival of another creature. Faluffel looked relieved and jumped up straight away.

"Oh, Owen," she squeaked in glee, "this is Ostracod. He is going to give us away."

Owen was thrilled with Ostracod: he could only be described as shaped rather like an old potato – one that had been left in a dark cupboard, for he had begun to sprout. Above and below his face grew two bunches of whiskers, which quivered as he spoke. His eye, a black spot rather like an 'eye' in a potato, but beady and intelligent, was placed near the top of his head and twinkled in a friendly way.

"How do you do," said Owen politely. "I'm Boy-animalcule Owen, Homo Sapiens."

"Growlywowly wowly grrr" ... came the reply ... which Owen took to mean: "I'm Ostracod. Cypris Reptans Ostracod. Good to see you." ... but he wasn't sure. However, Ostracod's expression was friendly enough.

They all swam down to the wedding ceremony, alighting on a leaf of a huge Water Milfoil plant, where Bosmina was waiting. Above and below them, on other leafy platforms, smiling creatures chattered together excitedly. Faluffel waved to Difflugia and some of the Protozoa opposite. She nodded politely to the Shrimps. Only Cyclops wasn't happy. She had sprawled herself on the platform in an ungainly heap. Then Ostracod tucked his arm through Faluffel's and started to lead her gently along a huge silken rope that was fixed to the stem, just below their platform. Sedilla, the other Maid of Honour, had to haul Cyclops to her feet before she would condescend to follow.

Owen sat transfixed. From their platform and from other strategic points of the Milfoil, fat silken ropes, glistening in the light, stretched down to support an enormous shining dome. It was a magnificent construction built entirely of finely-woven silk and shaped like an oriental onion-dome. They had not long to wait before there was a disturbance in the water. A hairy spider appeared with tiny silver bubbles clinging all over her body. She had come down from the surface carrying with her a larger bubble full of fresh air. This she released under her dome, causing it to wobble gently and enlarge still further.

Owen clutched at Daphnia's arm.

"Don't worry, that's Argyroneta, or Neta as we like to call her. She won't harm you. We're quite safe here. We've been waiting for her."

"But surely, she's not the one who is going to perform the ceremony?"

"Yes she is," said Bosmina. "I'll explain why she was chosen. In order to make her dome, which you must admit is the best construction in the Pond, she spins a flat sheet of pure watered silk, attaching this with threads to weeds at the place she has chosen to build. Then she collects bubbles of air from above the Green and releases them under her net. As the bubbles rise, they push the centre of the silken sheet upwards, as you've just seen."

"And when the bubble-dome is completed, as it nearly is now," said Daphnia, admiringly, "she will go inside and divide her home into two compartments. Her mate will be so impressed, he will instantly fall in love with her and the bubble-house."

"Then", Bosmina continued, "he will make love with her, and before long, Neta will go into her nursery to lay her eggs … fifty to a hundred of them. She'll keep an eye on them from the living-room until they're hatched. The important thing is, she won't spoil everything by eating her husband, as other spiders do. As a result they're considered to be the Pond's best example of marital bliss. That's why it's Neta's social duty to perform the wedding ceremony for other creatures; and she does it so well."

"Ssh! It's starting," said Daphnia. There was sudden hush. All eyes turned towards the silken ropes. Looking shy and pretty, Faluffel, escorted by Ostracod, had nearly reached Charles Copepod and his best man, Rottifer the Rotifer.

"I can see why Faluffel likes Charles," Owen thought. "He is very handsome."

Balanced beautifully on the rope, Charles held his dignified head erect. His two large antennae branched sideways and swept in a graceful curve down the whole length of his body. His body-segments were orange, red and black.

The bride and bridegroom met where two ropes crossed, and Charles took Faluffel's arm, while Ostracod waited behind with the two Maids of Honour.

"This is the difficult bit," whispered Daphnia, as the best man carried out his duty. Owen was entranced by Rottifer. He was small and funny and reminded Owen of his uncle. He was shaped like a tapered cylinder that ended in one foot. This in turn ended in two pointed toes that were balanced superbly on the rope.

Slowly and apprehensively he started to rotate along the rope that lead to Neta's dome, aided by an astonishing corona of vibrating hairs on the top of his head. The giant spider had stopped her work, and greeted the Rotifer when he finished rotating. Rottifer greeted her in return, asking for her gracious permission to perform the ceremony. No-one could hear the Rotifer's carefully prepared speech, but they saw Neta bow her head and move towards the pair.

"How I would hate to be best man," whispered Owen to Bosmina. "Rottifer is awfully brave."

"I know," said Bosmina. "That is why the best man has to be your very best friend. Hush now and wait."

The huge spider reached the couple and began binding them together with a silken thread.

"Bound together never to part," squeaked Sedilla solemnly.

The other Maid of Honour was meant to speak these words too, but instead she glowered.

Argyroneta's work was done. She turned and made her way back to the dome. Then the Rotifer took the sacred piece of pearly-pink shell that Ostracod picked up from the wedding-bowl, and cutting through the silken threads that bound them together said: "I now pronounce you man and wife."

There was a great deal of applause and the bride and groom were showered with hundreds of tiny coloured pebbles.

*In the middle of the clearing, arranged along
the entire length of a large flattened boulder,
was a magnificent Pond-feast.*

9

THE FEAST

There was a lull now on the platform as the ceremony ended. The whole Pond was filled with creatures threading their way through the silken ropes and swaying weeds as they swam off in different directions. The small group of Faluffel's friends gathering to go down for the feast waved as the other guests departed. Owen was introduced to Charles who shook hands politely and bowed low; then to Rottifer the Rotifer, a wheel-animalcule. "Charmed to meet you. Charmed indeed." His voice seemed to unwind itself from the depth of his insides. Daphnia said she was simply dying for the feast and wanted to start straight away. Laughing at her relish for food, Faluffel consented. She felt so happy. Everything had gone well.

Charles led the party down to the Bottom. He swam gracefully, his long antennae balanced at right-angles. Beside him, Faluffel hopped happily. Behind Owen and Sedilla, Cyclops leapt through the water with no style at all. Beyond her, Ostracod swam energetically, his whiskers whirling away like clockwork. Next to him, the Rotifer rotated with great speed and, way behind them all, Bosmina towed Daphnia along by her arm. Daphnia looked like a barge being pulled along by a tug. They were talking nineteen to the dozen about the wonderful wedding.

In this pleasant manner they made their way through the Pelagic zone. The lower they swam the greater the buzz of activity, as everyone hurried about cheerfully attending to their business.

Owen decided he liked this part of the Pond most. It was light and full of tall weeds, all trying to reach the surface. He could tell the ones that got there as they had stopped growing upwards and had settled down to thicken their stems and produce side branches. Soon the wedding guests were swimming over the mossy meadow. It was afternoon and in the hot Sun many more bubbles were being formed. They filled the whole valley making it twinkle with prisms of light. Pond creatures milled around them, covering the landscape as far as they could see.

Swimming west, they came eventually to an area where large pebble-boulders interrupted the carpet of mossy sphagnum in the manner of a Chinese landscape. Some of the boulders were standing on their heads, some sideways. Over these stone surfaces, Pond-weeds, Water-Milfoil and Stone-worts in an array of colours were clinging with long spreading roots. In the middle of the clearing, arranged along the entire length of a large flattened boulder, was a magnificent Pond-feast. Grisella, Bosmina's cousin, had been guarding it for them, and Charles invited her to join them.

The table was loaded with the prettiest, most colourful shapes and looked so splendid, it was met by a series of high squeaks, low growls and gurgling noises from everyone. Jellies, trifles and party food above the Green were nothing, absolutely nothing, compared with the food here. There were bright blue wriggly things, star-shaped green things, and hollow pods filled with long yellow filaments of spaghetti-stuff, fine red strands and green zig-zag threads.

Grisella bade them all be seated, and after saying "Ready, steady, go," the feast was attacked with vehemence. Everyone tried to help themselves to vast heaps of Algae all at once, ladling the heaps into mountains in front of them and encouraging them towards their mouths with their arms. Owen helped himself to a large yellow diatom. It tasted delicious; like a cross between gooseberry jelly and banana custard. After that he crunched a blue desmid. That was like a mixture of melon and Turkish delight. Then he tried a pod full of red strands which looked just like red spaghetti. To his surprise, they tasted just like red spaghetti too. Without knives and forks and table-manners, eating spaghetti was great fun.

After a time the creatures paused, while Charles and Faluffel opened their wedding presents.

"A lovely silken hammock," squeaked Faluffel.

"A marvellously-special pebble." Charles smiled.

"A set of hollow pods. Just exactly what we wanted."

"And I have a present for you too," said Owen.

He had opened up his spectacle case and drew out the paper-clip. No-one would want that. But it was too late: Faluffel jumped from her place, rushed round and leaned over his shoulder.

"Ooh," she gasped, "Whatever is that silvery shiny thing so cleverly bent up like that?"

"It's a paper-clip," said Owen, feeling embarrassed and trying to put it back. But Faluffel had already grabbed it.

"A clip. A clip. I've always wanted a paper-clip." She studied it for some time.

"It is for going round my neck, isn't it?"

"Yes, that's what it's for," said Owen quickly. "And it's hung onto this piece of string."

There was another gasp as the string was drawn out. Charles took the string and threaded it through the paper-clip. Faluffel had gone pink with excitement. Owen knotted the string to the correct length and presented it to Charles. Faluffel hung her head down so that Charles could put it round her neck. There was a silence as the ceremony was carried out; then everybody cheered.

But Cyclops had always wanted a paper-clip too, it seemed. Her eye glowered with jealousy and she trembled and shook with rage.

"You look very pretty, my dear," said Charles tenderly to Faluffel.

"Nonsense," croaked Cyclops snidely. "You're just infatuated with her so-called beauty. She won't look after you very well. She's just a child."

"My dear sister, calm yourself, do," beseeched Charles. He looked hurt.

"You'll be back with me in a day or two, you'll see," Cyclops continued.

"How dare you." Faluffel had gone red with anger. She looked at Charles, but he was eating hard. Sedilla had warned him beforehand that it was better to put up with all manner of insults than to let Cyclops lose her temper. But there was a loud squeak from Cyclops, so something must have happened behind the table. Her hands began writhing and her feet twitched in spasms. Her eye blazed with hatred, first at Faluffel and then at Charles.

"Charles will soon be bored on a honeymoon with you and will want to come home."

"How could he be, we're going to see the Frog's Spawn."

There was a cry of delight and envy from everyone down the table, but Cyclops had gone scarlet. She leapt to her feet, formed her arms into little round fists, and banged them down hard on the table.

"You promised you'd take *me* to the Spawn one day. Now you're going without me. You'll regret this!" she screamed, her face quivering.

Charles was about to pacify her again when Faluffel got up and pushed him back into his seat. She looked flushed, but very determined. She gripped the pod in front of her with both arms and threw it through the water at Cyclops. The pod hit her face and its contents spilled all over her head.

"Leave us alone!" she shouted. "I won't have you spoiling our happiness any longer. Charles has put up with you long enough. Now it's our turn."

The others were stunned. None of them would ever have dared speak to Cyclops in that way. They were all far too scared of her. Yet Faluffel had said what many of them had wanted to say for ages. Cyclops looked round expecting someone to apologise on Faluffel's behalf, but no one flinched. Then she turned deathly white and without further ado swam furiously away.

"Faluffel, you were grr ... grr ... great," said Ostracod.

"My dear, what courage," said Daphnia.

"I've been dying to do that for ages," said Bosmina in her high tremolo voice.

"Blurp, I think you were very brave, Blurp," said Rottifer.

Only Charles and Sedilla exchanged frightened glances. There would be repercussions. From now on they'd better all watch out.

The others, oblivious of their fears, set to feasting again with renewed vigour. Daphnia ate large mouthfuls in quick succession, marshalling the food towards her mouth with her two long feathery arms. Grisella ate politely but with reserve after what had happened. Ostracod concentrated on crunching a blue diatom with his powerful mandibles, emitting low growls between each mouthful. The Rotifer ate so hard his corona of hairs had to waft a rush of water downwards to cool his brow as well as filter food into his mouth. As he ate, his two disc-like eyes grew larger and larger and his cylindrical body expanded into a barrel-shape. Eventually Sedilla too began to eat. Soon Charles relaxed, putting one of his spare arms on Faluffel's shell. He had excellent table manners, taking little bits of everything which he filtered into his mouth with his maxilliped.

He paid great attention to Faluffel, proudly passing her this and that in a gentlemanly way. Her heroic action had made him love and respect her all the more.

The wedding guests were nearly full now. Owen could tell simply by observing the state of the water-fleas' insides. He could see through their transparent bodies right into their middles. There was a mixture of all the different Algae they had eaten, bedded down into coloured layers.

"I perceive that you can eat a little more, Daphnia dear," said Bosmina. "Do let me help you to some of the green."

After the feast had ended there was a great deal of bulging and belching and cleaning of whiskers The ladies tidied their arms and antennae simply by wafting them around in the water until they were shiny and clean. The gentlemen shook their whiskers and coughed slightly. Then they all arose and left the boulder, to wave Charles and Faluffel off on their honeymoon. And there was no washing up to do because all the food had been eaten, the boulder had washed itself clean, and two small bugs had already clambered onto the table to inspect the empty pods to see if they would make suitable homes.

The great Pond Snail was bending over them all,
and it was his expression of unhappiness
that Owen and Sedilla first noticed.

10

THE KIDNAP

Sedilla said she would swim Owen safely back to his jar. The wedding was over, and as they swam along in the fading light, they fell into a contented silence. They passed over the Protozoa and could dimly see Volvox, settled down for the night behind a stone, and later Difflugia, withdrawn into her shell. They swam through the bicycle entrance and saw the Great Pond Snail, his shell burnished to a deep purple in the last rays of the Sun. Then Owen had an idea, and by the time his Jar came into view, he had had carefully opened his glasses-case without the contents floating away, and found his lucky 5p coin. Secretly he wrapped it in the handkerchief.

"Sedilla, this is a special present for you. It's called a 5p. Don't open it till you get back. Good night."

"Thank you, Owen, very much. And I promise to come and fetch you tomorrow." Her face glowed as she brushed her feathery arm lightly across his cheek.

Owen was awakened by Sedilla tapping on his glass jar.

"Thank you for you precious gifts," she said as she stepped inside. "I made a pillow out of the white square and slept on it all night. It's nice to have your initials written on the corner. And you'll never guess where I've put the 5p." She turned around, and there it was, shining among her eggs, lying neatly with them in her pouch.

"What a good idea, Sedilla. It looks beautiful there."

"Today I'm going to show you how to help in the Pond," Sedilla announced as they swam towards the Centre. "First I have to teach some swimming, then encourage little creatures that are having difficulty in hatching, and lastly help to rebuild a house that has been pulled down by a marauding Dragonfly larva. You'll soon be able to do your own work, but it's a question of looking to see where you can help and, more important, which ones are the dangerous ones."

Owen was pleased to be allowed to help, but confused about something Sedilla had said earlier.

"But I still don't understand, Sedilla, why you said we should be selfish and enjoy ourselves all the time. Isn't it being *un*-selfish, helping all these people?"

"Now I don't understand *you*. Surely you enjoy a marvellous feeling of self-satisfaction, a glowing inside when you do something for someone else? Haven't you felt that when you put yourself out for another?"

Owen thought hard, and the more he thought, the less he remembered having put himself out for anyone, above the Green. How thoughtless he must have been. Sometimes he even wondered why his own twin, Bethan, put up with him, as he often relied on her to help him. He could hardly bear it. How he longed to help in the Pond; then he would be accepted as a permanent Pond-creature instead of just a visitor from above the Green.

They had almost reached the City Walls when they saw the small group of creatures standing round something on the ground. The great Pond Snail was bending over them all, and it was his expression of unhappiness that Owen and Sedilla first noticed.

By the time they reached the small gathering, all eyes were turned towards them, including those of Daphnia, Bosmina, Rottifer and Ostracod, and a path was made for them to walk right through to the centre.

"Oh! Poor Charles!" Sedilla choked. "Whatever have they done to you?"

Charles's antennae, once so finely spread, were bruised and crushed and fell limply over his shoulders. His highly-coloured segments were scratched and torn in several places and he had obviously lost a lot of fluid. On his face was a look of such utter dejection that it had set hard and he no longer had the will to speak. Sedilla bent down, gently took his arm, and with her own feathery one brushed aside a torn piece that hung down, obscuring his right eye. She began gently calling his name.

Charles's mouth opened and he tried to form words, but nothing came out. Then suddenly he began to speak, as though it was difficult to form his thoughts.

"Faluffel. She's gone. Been taken. My pretty wife. My Faluffel."

"Taken? What do you mean, Charles. You must try to explain."

Charles opened his eyes and stared at Sedilla blankly.

"My sister, Cyclops. After all I've done for her. She followed us as we went on our honeymoon, as if she wanted to come too."

"The wretched creature. We shouldn't have trusted her. Where has she taken Faluffel? We must go and get her at once," said Sedilla firmly.

"I don't know."

And he hid his face in his antennae.

"Charles, what exactly did happen? You must tell us quickly before it's too late."

"We went to sleep on a little leaf of Milfoil weed. It was too dark to start along the Ridge that leads to the Spawn, so we stopped just before it. When I awoke, she wasn't there."

Charles broke down with grief.

"But did you check your own home, in case she'd been taken back there?"

"Yes, but she wasn't there, and the place was surrounded with my sister's Copepod friends … they said she'd promised them positions of power when she gained control. They were the ones who did this to me. They were waiting for me. They accused my friends of killing one of their gang. I called them liars and said I knew nothing of it. I barely got away with my life."

"Oh, Charles," said Sedilla, remembering the mobbing, "yes there was a Copepod killed just before the wedding, but it was in self defence. They attacked us first. I didn't want to tell you of it because it would have ruined your wedding day."

"But how do you know it was Cyclops who took Faluffel, and not the Copepods?" interrupted Daphnia.

"Because of the message," said Charles, now sobbing uncontrollably.

"The message?" said everybody. "What message?"

"When I woke up: there, pinned to the leaf with this long sharp spine, was a message scratched on a smaller leaf. It said: 'I have taken her to my special place. I will dispose of her unless you return to me alone.' It was signed 'C.'"

"But that sharp spine looks like one of Heliozoa's spiny spicules, surely? And your sister's 'special place' must be a place where she used to go. Try to remember, Charles, please."

"My mind is too confused. I know there was a place where she used to meet her Copepod friends; but she never told me where and she never let me go there."

"But someone must know. Please think. Think for all you are worth." Sedilla propped him up and wafted a current of water over his face to cool it down.

"There is one person, a friend of ours. She used to feel sorry for Cyclops and talk to her. Difflugia. That's who it was. But she's disappeared. All the Protozoa are hidden. I remember now. I tried to find one on my way here."

"Then there's no time to lose!" cried Sedilla. "Everybody must help. Fan out and look for both Faluffel and Difflugia. Try to get information from the other creatures. But be discreet. Only ask our friends. I'll stay here with Charles. If anyone hears or sees anything, come straight back. Bosmina, Daphnia, search by the outskirts and Nurseries; Rottifer, all round the Centre. Ostracod, all through the Pelagic zone, and Owen up by the Green and even above it as that's your territory. Go now, all of you, and take care."

The friends quickly dispersed. Owen swam fast, looking for the giant Burweed, around which the bubbles would collect before exploding above the Green. He found it easily. It was the biggest plant in the whole Pond. Its gigantic trunk was composed of bundles of tubes packed tightly together. Gurgling noises came from inside the tubes where all sorts of juices welled up or rushed down. Around it spread great roots sticking out like elbows through the moss.

Owen jumped into the first bubble that formed below it, and up he went, keeping a good look-out all around. But instead of breaking through the surface, the bubble exploded, sending him spinning down. Owen realized he would have to catch a bubble that was travelling up right next to the trunk. This worked better. The bubble seemed most adept at avoiding the leaves and branches in its eagerness to reach the top. Half way up, the bubble hit and lodged underneath a long curling leaf directly over its path and Owen almost cried with frustration.

He was about to dive out and start all over again, when he

thought of a good plan. Couldn't he dislodge the bubble himself simply by banging hard against the bubble-sides with his back? He began to do this. Sure enough the bubble started to shift along the underside of the leaf. It had almost reached the edge, when Owen, looking out, came face to face with a terrible bright red beetle face. It stared at Owen through the bubble wall with two revolving eyes and waved the two creepy-crawly antennae which stuck out from its head.

Slowly it grasped the bubble with its two horny arms. Owen cringed. The thing would prise open the bubble and eat him.

Then looking through the bubble-floor, he saw that the beetle was only the top half of a hatching larvae. The bottom part was still tucked into its soft green cocoon attached to the leaf.

Fortunately Owen would still be able to escape if he dived out the other side of the bubble. But to his amazement he found that the beetle face had changed expression and was now grinning playfully and gurgling at the back of its throat.

Before Owen had time to summon up a smile in return, there was a resounding thwack and the larva had shucked the bottom of its cocoon, giving the bubble a hefty blow from underneath. Immediately the bubble dislodged itself and spun upwards.

At the surface, it managed to push itself through the skin and stick to some other bubbles that were forming in a large mass, supported against the stem of the Burweed. Owen found himself completely enclosed in a bubble paradise. There were half-bubbles, quarter-bubbles, double-bubbles and tiny bubbles too small to get inside.

The brightness was so intense that Owen's head hurt and he had to close his eyes. When he could open them again, instead of all the Green, there above him was a familiar sight. His own world: a sky of bright blue and in it a morning sun. A few fluffy white clouds made their way across the sky. But the scenery that surrounded him – the crown of the giant Burweed, the White Crowfoot petals and the other weeds that managed to break through the Green – was huge, and Owen was minute. Below him was the surface skin stretched taut over the Pond rather like a sheet of filmy plastic. On it were creatures sliding along at great speed as though taking part in some huge skating ballet. On the noisy mirror floor, whirligig beetles spun round and round, their shiny black shells glinting in silver and purple streaks. Springtails leapt high into the air. The giant water strider slid over the surface in zig-zag patterns, occasionally making terrific leaps, and between them all, the raft spider ran hither and thither at startling speeds, dazzling in the spotlight of the sun.

Owen was mesmerised by their dizzy movement, and below the water-film he saw, too, the black mosquito-wigglers stretching and bending in their ugly rhythmic dance. His head reeled in confusion. Which world did he belong to? Above or below the Green? He didn't know. Then through the whirling in his head, Owen heard a voice calling him. A squeaking voice pleading: "Owen. Owen."

It was Faluffel, trapped somewhere very near. Owen pushed his way through the bubbles until he reached the further side of the Burweed. And he became aware of a gentle tapping accompanying the voice … like someone hammering a tack into a piece of wood. At first he couldn't tell its direction, as it made a hollow sound that echoed all around; but as it grew louder and more insistent he saw that it came from a pale brown case stuck to a stem of Burweed, close by. The case looked like an Egyptian Mummy, for it was dry and hard, covered in strange ridges and marks.

The sounds increased, becoming urgent, and to his dismay, Owen realized that they came from inside the case. Could Faluffel be imprisoned there? Owen's heart beat faster and he pressed his ear against the bubble wall. But he heard the squeaks turn to groans full of effort and struggle, and instead of "Owen, Owen" they were crying "Oh when? Oh when? Oh when can I be free?"

Suddenly, as he watched, the case gave a great heave and split open all the way down one side. Instead of Faluffel, a pair of mandibles appeared through the crust and started to crunch until they had bitten out a round hole. From this hole a head emerged; a shiny brown horny head with a compound eye. Owen stared. The case split further behind the thorax, as the rest of the body appeared. The groans of agony scared Owen: he remained transfixed until the whole creature, its abdomen and a pair of crumpled damp wings, had crawled out onto the top of its case. It was a fly-thing, shiny and new. Now it stood silent and still, waiting for its wings to dry. As they hardened and unfurled, the membraneous wings filled with sparkling colours. All at once the fly was no longer there. It had flown away, skimming low over the water, leaving its hard brown case behind.

For several minutes Owen couldn't move, but sat shivering on the bubble floor. It wasn't until the mass of bubbles decided to rearrange itself and Owen was sent tumbling through into the one beneath that he remembered where he was. Shaken into action, he found himself diving quickly through the bubbles, piercing one wall after another until finally he plunged through the surface-skin and past the evil wigglers.

Guiltily he realized which world needed him the most.

Carefully he searched beneath the Green, desperately trying to make up for lost time. He had almost reached the White Crowfoot when he was rudely shoved aside by a small Shrimp.

Instead of the Shrimp apologising, Owen found his ear being

nipped and a harsh voice whispering urgently:

"I come from Mysis Relicta. He says he knows where Difflugia is, and that you'll want to know."

"Yes, yes. Tell me quickly."

"She's hiding under the Pond-sponges, below the City walls." And the Shrimp was off in a flash, before Owen had time to thank him.

Owen glided fast towards the bicycle walls. He rushed headlong through the gates, straight to where Sedilla sat, still rocking Charles's head in her lap.

"Sedilla. Sedilla. Difflugia's here. Right next to us, hiding beneath the Pond-sponge walls."

Although she thought she had camouflaged herself well, Difflugia had left the tip of one of her jelloid toes sticking out from beneath her shell, and it didn't take long for Sedilla to spot her. She tapped and beseeched until Difflugia peered out from under her basin and started to uncurl. She had been crying. Her eyes were red; her face looked huddled and sad.

When she extended her jelloid legs, they sagged and her beautiful shell, with its bits and pieces stuck all over, seemed too heavy for her to hold up. In a muffled voice she began:

"They've killed the Sun-animalcule Heliozoa. Crushed all his spines. He died from shock."

"Oh, poor Heliozoa. How could they do that to him?" Sedilla was grief-stricken.

"For killing one of their gang. The Heliozoa meant no harm. He was just protecting you. Now he's dead and we're afraid."

With that, Difflugia curled up and started to retract into her shell.

"So that's why the Protozoa are in hiding. No, Difflugia, wait. Don't go. You have to help us, please. Faluffel's life is at stake. You don't want her to die as well?"

"All right. What do you want to know?" Difflugia looked up from under the brim of her basin.

"Cyclops has taken Faluffel to her special place. Besides the Copepods, you're the only one who knows where that is."

Sedilla stroked the two jelloid feet and tapped gently at the shell.

"I'll tell you then, but you must travel fast if you want to save her. Cyclops has a cave on the Bottom, over on the left of the Ridge. Just beyond the Dragonfly larvae. Leave me now and go."

Owen and Sedilla raced back to Charles. He had recovered slightly and wanted to go to the cave with them, but the Pond Snail wouldn't hear of it.

"You're in no fit state. You'd die if you went."

"Then listen to me," said Charles, raising himself up onto his arms. "If you do manage to rescue my Faluffel, tell her to meet me at Bear's Bucket. They say the Spawn is just above his place this year. As soon as I can get to my feet I'll ask Rottifer and Ostracod to escort me there – and another thing, send her my love and tell her to be brave."

"I promise. Owen and I will set out straight away ..."

"The Ridge is no place for a Boy-animalcule to go," warned the Great Pond Snail. "It's better he should stay behind."

"He is right," said Charles. "Owen, you are not to go. You know nothing of the dangers ... and here, take this along with you, Sedilla ... Heliozoa's sharp spicule for protection. He would have wanted a bit of himself to be useful to you, whom he so much admired."

Owen turned to Sedilla. "If you don't let me come with you to rescue Faluffel, I'll leave the Pond."

They looked at one another. Sedilla was torn. She didn't want Owen to leave, nor did she want to travel alone.

There was a silence, broken by the Snail.

"Listen, if you two don't set out soon, there'll be no Faluffel to save. *You* must swim in front, Sedilla, as you know the dangerous creatures. Owen *you* must follow closely behind."

Bidding farewell to Charles and the Snail, they swam off through the bicycle gate. First Sedilla headed in the direction of Owen's Jam Jar Palace; then turning left, plunged deeper into the Pond. She'd been to the Ridge only once before and had to ponder the way carefully. She'd heard conflicting tales from creatures who had been along the Ridge and didn't know which to believe. Some described majestic colours and wondrous landscapes: those who had seen the Spawn said it was the most astonishing spectacle they had ever witnessed. Others told of terrors which one dared not listen to: tales of Pond-ghosts; witches with green hair; weaving snakes and moving jellies that sucked their victims dry. Although Sedilla no longer looked scared, inside she was deeply afraid.

Out from behind a rock wobbled a large leaf-shaped jelly
with nothing visible except for her two eyes and some pale brown eggs
that made lines of spots down each of her sides.

PART 2

11

THE GIANT TRANSPARENT BLOB

The water pressed cold about Owen and Sedilla as they travelled deeper. Mudbanks took over from weeds, oxygen became scarce, making the atmosphere stagnant and sour, and swimming became an effort. As the Pond grew darker, gloom spread over everything, living and dead alike, embracing rocks and caverns with wretched despair. Pondering was difficult so that Sedilla felt uncertain of the way. She had to ask several reliable-looking creatures to direct them to the 'Red Place', which she knew marked the start of the Ridge. Eventually a small beetle put them right and, swimming on, they soon saw a strange red glow in the distance. It filtered through the water, enveloping them in its colour as they arrived. Sedilla looked livid and hot-tempered, Owen feverish and scorched.

The colour came from crimson moss covering the ground and red Algae stretched over the surface of the rocks, creeping finger-like with slimy threads. The Algae tangled into knots around the dark brown Pond-weed, and piled into heaps upon the stones. Among these coils that stank of decay they saw the water Hog-louse, the giant Isopod, rooting his way through the Detritus on the Bottom. He made satisfied grunting noises as he ate the putrefying matter.

Sedilla and Owen swam low over the red landscape. They passed hundreds of scarlet gnat larvae tucked into their tubes, waving their heads to one another, nodding in a brainless fashion. These lulled the swimmers into such a sluggish motion that they were unaware of the two approaching Mites.

"Quick Owen, swim higher!" Sedilla ordered.

Owen suddenly realised the dangers of this deeper part of the Pond. With clawed feet and crimson hairy legs, the two mites clambered through the slimy weed, hidden until the last moment by their camouflage.

"Diplodontus Despiciens," whisperd Sedilla. "They are bloodsuckers; some of the most despicable members of the Pond. We'll have to swim higher from now on."

Pond-creatures slowly dwindled in number. Those who travelled past, eyed Owen and Sedilla warily, keeping to the safety of the shadows till they had gone by. They swam over colonies of red worms, wriggling below in the mud, swarming and locked together in groups. But Owen took no notice of the worms. He had become aware of something in the distance; a noise like the chomping and chewing of hundreds of hungry alligators. The noise cut sharply through the water, splitting into small echoes as it rebounded from the rocks.

"Beware, we're approaching the Dragonfly larvae," warned Sedilla. "Watch for their jaws. They shoot them out, hook you onto their pincers and draw you back into their mouths. They are such voracious eaters they'll eat almost anything … even one another if they have a mind to."

The red area faded behind them and brown troubled water took its place. As they passed over the Dragonfly larvae, the snapping noises became deafening. Owen dared himself to look down. What he saw horrified him. Long segmented bodies thrust their brown stick-like legs in a cannibalistic dance. From the huge heads, mandibles slashed at the water, sharp and cruel.

"Uggh! I'm glad I can swim!" Owen shouted.

"But we may have to walk soon," Sedilla shouted back. "I didn't want to tell you, but I'm sure I've seen some Stickleback shapes swimming above."

Beyond the Dragonfly larvae they reached a sandy area.

"Owen, see what's in front of us. You'll love these creatures," Sedilla said, thankful to forget the snapping noises behind. She pointed excitedly to some extraordinary creatures ahead of them. "These are the Caddis larvae. They're completely harmless and the most brilliant architects. They use practically anything with which to build their cases. They all compete to see who can build the tallest, most artfully designed houses."

The larvae-cases were built from small sticks and stalks welded together; tiny round fragments of sand; rough pieces of shell; leaves wrapped, twisted or turned spirally to form cylinders.

"Oh look," said Owen. "That poor larva is hunting everywhere for a long narrow bit to fit the hole in his case. How do they find their bits and pieces?"

"They can walk about with their heads and legs protruding from the front of their cases, looking for material as they go. If danger threatens, like fish arriving, they withdraw their feet and heads pretending they aren't there. The fish can swallow them whole though, case and all ... listen Owen, if you want to watch them for a while, stay here treading water. Difflugia said that Cyclops' cave was just beyond the Dragonfly larvae. These creatures are reliable so I'll go and ask around for directions."

While Sedilla was gone, Owen watched the Caddis, fascinated.

Through the sediment he could see that they had even used bits of other Pond-creatures for their cases. Old antennae, cast off chitinous cases or small pieces of skeleton had been neatly cemented together. Complete snail-shells had been used and several, he noticed, still contained live snails.

Suddenly Owen had a brilliant idea … a helpful idea. He swam down towards the Caddis that had been looking for a long narrow piece to fit his case. As Owen approached, the Caddis withdrew his waving arms and head into his case. But after Owen had knocked politely on his house, a very small area of head, patterned attractively in geometric designs of yellow and brown, appeared over the top, followed by a friendly wrinkled eye which questioned him nervously.

"I thought you might need my pencil," said Owen. "I'm sure it will fit the large slit in your house nicely."

Owen opened his glasses-case carefully, drew out the pencil and tried it for size, being careful not to let it float away. It fitted perfectly.

"Thank you," said the Caddis in his broken crackly voice. "It fits just right," and he began cementing the pencil into place. It looked splendid.

"Well, I have to go now," and Owen waved, swimming happily away. Now he had helped someone in the Pond, he felt very satisfied.

He was enjoying this new feeling so much that he swam higher than he meant to; and before he realised his mistake, saw not one or two, but three dark shapes change course and make towards him.

"Sedilla!" he yelled in panic, and dived desperately, not daring to see if the shapes were following.

He swam downwards until he reached the darkness, then hid under a stone on the Bottom.

After a while, when he considered it safe, he turned and made his way back onto the Ridge where he thought Sedilla had gone. But she wasn't there, or any-where else that he looked. Eventually he sat down on the Bottom. He was lost.

Owen was no longer afraid of the dark shapes, because the only thing he wanted in the whole world was Sedilla. Without her, the Pond felt very empty.

When he heard the "co-eee" coming from the centre of the glade that stretched out ahead, he was confused. It sounded very like Sedilla, and yet it didn't. But when it called for the second time, he jumped with joy and started to make his way towards it.

"Sedilla, coo-eee!"

"Coo-eee," came the answer. Even if it wasn't Sedilla, the voice sounded friendly enough, so he decided to ask whoever it might be the way back onto the Ridge. But although the glade was open and relatively clear, there was no-one to be seen.

Only a few coarse rocks jutted out from the mudflats that spread on either side. The vegetation was so sparse that the way seemed safe enough. As he ran on, however, the atmosphere grew dismal and strangely oppressive. His feet started to drag through the mud and grow heavier with every tread. The emptiness made him uneasy. He was about to turn round and wade back, when a voice, very near, boomed a greeting. Out from behind a rock wobbled a large leaf-shaped jelly with nothing visible except for her two eyes and some pale brown eggs that made lines of spots down each of her sides.

"How delightful to see you," she said to Owen. "You perfectly gorgeous little creature. Let me embrace you. I'm Mesostoma, the giant transparent Blob. Couldn't you see me calling you?"

"How could I? You're transparent except for your line of spots," he answered sullenly. He was disappointed she wasn't Sedilla.

"Yes, of course, how silly of me," she gushed, and wobbled closer to Owen, rippling her frilly edges and making as if to throw herself into his arms. But Owen retreated, feeling uneasy.

"Can you please tell me the way back onto the Ridge? I'm lost."

"Over there, of course," she rippled her frill towards the wood behind. Owen turned to see where she was pointing, but as he looked, Mesostoma wobbled forwards and began to fold him in a rapturous embrace. Owen shuddered as the cold jelly hugged him close. Tighter and tighter she squeezed until he realized what was happening. She was trying to squeeze him to death! Immediately he began to fight her off, throwing out his arms and legs and digging in with his elbows. There seemed to be jelly everywhere pushing down on his head and face, slowly suffocating him. She was trying to prevent him moving at all. He made an effort to escape. Almost choked, he jabbed her hard with his knees and heels; then clawed frantically at her jelly. But his fingernails sank uselessly into her rubbery body. Now he couldn't breathe anywhere over his body.

He was about to struggle for the last time when he stopped himself. There was just one way which might work. Suddenly he went completely slack. Mesostoma, thinking she had overpowered her victim, released her hold on him a little. With his remaining strength, Owen gave one mighty wrench, and broke free. Keeping low over the mud, he raced as fast as he could towards the protection of the wood. He could hear the giant Blob laughing behind him across the glade as he ploughed through the sluggish water. But when he came to the wood and was about to plunge in through the weeds, he swam slap into some sticky transparent ropes that had been carefully fixed as a trap.

The more Owen struggled to free himself, the faster he became entangled in the slimy ropes. He felt like a fly caught in a spider's web. Defeated, he stopped struggling and resigned himself to his fate. He had already seen Mesostoma wobbling slowly towards him. She was in no hurry. She had obviously tricked him about the way back to the Ridge. She was certainly making quite sure that if her victims avoided her embrace they would still not be able to leave her glade. She could now eat him at her leisure. Parcelled in the sticky web, she would suck him like the spider sucks the fly.

Then Owen saw that Mesostoma had stopped pursuing him. To his dismay, he saw the reason why. There was Sedilla, walking straight towards the Blob, following a call that sounded like a copy of his own voice. She would have been almost transparent herself if it wasn't for a small shining circle of silver that glittered from her pouch.

"Sedilla!" He screamed as loud as he could. "Don't let her near you. Don't let her embrace you. It's Mesostoma, the giant transparent Blob!"

Sedilla was confused. Owen's voice seemed to be coming from every direction. She hesitated, not knowing what to do, and in that moment, Mesostoma plunged towards Sedilla, wrapped herself around her and folded her frills tightly together. Then drawing Sedilla inwards against her middle, she squeezed tighter and tighter. Owen watched helplessly, knowing there was nothing he could do.

To see the person he loved hugged to death in front of him was more than he could bear. Again he tried to struggle out of the thick slimy threads but only tangled himself more, until they smothered his yells.

What Owen couldn't see from his position, was that Sedilla held Heliozoa's spiny spicule tightly in her feathery arms. What he didn't know – but what Sedilla did … was that although Mesostoma had her eyes and face on the top of her jelloid form, her soft mouth was in her middle. Mesostoma was about to bite Sedilla and suck her dry, when Heliozoa's spicule plunged into her mouth. The harder Mesostoma squeezed, the faster she caused her own death. Anywhere else on her jelloid body, the spicule would have been no more than a pin-prick, but here, at her most vulnerable spot, it proved fatal.

Meostoma gave a scream: a great gelatinous cry that echoed again and again through the empty glade. Staggering backwards, she unfolded her frill and let Sedilla go. Then she curled her frill over her own body and shivered with agony.

Surprised to be free, Sedilla stumbled along towards the direction of the other voice, still gripping the spicule. As she walked, she slowly became unsqueezed and her circulation came back to normal. She began to swim, painfully at first, then more strongly as she recognised the true Owen and saw his plight.

Sedilla turned to make sure she wasn't pursued, and saw a pitiful sight. Mesostoma had completely curled around herself and was collapsed in a shapeless jelly on the ground. The second time Sedilla looked round, the shapeless mass was pulsating rapidly. The third time, her pulse had weakened and her wobble was leaving her. Finally, as Sedilla reached Owen, they both saw the Blob stiffen and grow opaque. They knew then that they were safe from her as she was a jelly no more.

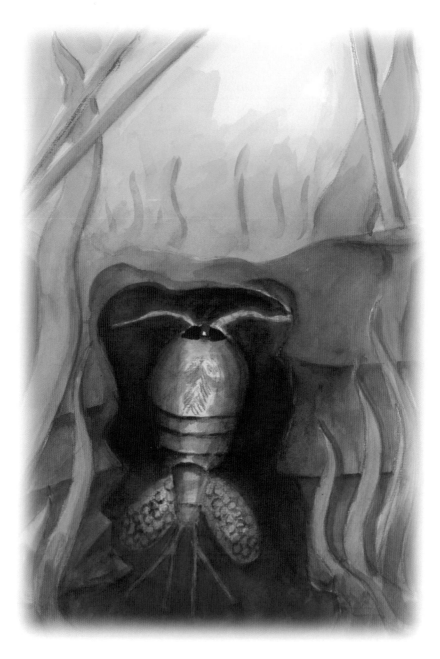

*"A narrow path that leads to Cyclops' cave. They say
she's gone mad and jumps out at everyone that passes."*
"Cyclops' cave!" they both shouted.

12

Cyclops' Cave

Carefully Sedilla sawed through the sticky threads from Owen's body. As she worked, she told him about her frantic search, and how it had been the same Caddis who had, in the end, directed her to where he had disappeared. She showed no anger towards him for disobeying her orders and Owen felt a great tenderness for her.

"Thank you for finding me again and sawing me free. I'm so glad you had the spicule and knew about Mesostoma's mouth. Do you feel unsqueezed yet?"

"Yes thank you. It wasn't so bad really; just a strange sensation to be hugged by a jelly. Sort of wobbly and smooth, rather shivery and cold."

"Yes", laughed Owen, as his last sticky threads were cut through.

But then they heard a wail of despair and, turning round, saw a ghastly giant green Blob trembling with anger over the dead lump that was Mesostoma.

"Oh no," said Sedilla in panic. "That must be Dalyella Viridis, Mesostoma's cousin. Quick, we must get away before she sees us."

"I'll get you for this. I'll get you even if it's the last thing I do. Wretches! Murderers!"

Sedilla took one look at the advancing viridian Blob and, diving through the hole Sedilla had made cutting him free, they plunged into the weed forest.

For ages they pushed past stems and wriggled through weeds until they felt far enough away from the Blob. Finally they collapsed exhausted on the ground.

"We're both lost now," said Sedilla in a small voice.

"Yes," said Owen quietly. "But I feel very found again now you're here."

"Then shall we be together from now on all the time?"

"Yes, I'd love that," said Owen feeling warm all over. "Now I really feel part of the Pond."

Linking arms, they walked through the dark weeds, intending to skirt round the outside and back to the Ridge. Soon they came across three small snails who were totally engrossed in eating their way through the wood.

"Please excuse us interrupting your meal, but could you tell us how to get onto the Ridge?"

"The way to the Ridge," one of the snails answered very slowly, "Is back the way you came."

"But we've just been chased from there. We can't possibly go that way."

"Well I don't advise you to go onwards. The Edge curves all round there and Furry Monsters abound. Above," he said, pointing with his horns, "are the black shapes. They swim so low over this part of the Pond that I don't advise you to swim at all. The only other way I cannot advise either."

"Which is that?" Owen asked.

"A narrow path that leads to Cyclops' cave. They say she's gone mad and jumps out at everyone that passes."

"Cyclops' cave!" they both shouted. "Thank you, that's just where we *do* want to go. Goodbye." And they swam off down the rocky brown path.

"Then mind the guards. Mind the two Copepod guards," the snails cried behind them.

The rocks were jagged and jutted sharply on either side. Above, the swirling shapes of Sticklebacks darted here and there, casting flickering shadows over them. Low against the Bottom, Owen and Sedilla swam side by side, keeping a sharp look-out for the guards.

Eventually, as they were rounding a corner, they spotted them: two fat Copepods standing before a small black cave. They would have been caught easily if the snails hadn't warned them. Quickly they slipped behind a rock. From the cave, eerie sounds emerged that made them tremble: low moans, high-pitched cackles of laughter; snatches of disjointed song, then silence.

"Poor Faluffel. I wonder if she's still alive?" Sedilla sobbed.

"Listen, I've thought of a plan," said Owen, "I'll creep round to the entrance and try to slip in while you distract the guard by banging stones against a rock."

Sedilla thought this too dangerous but, unable to think of another way, she had to agree. So while Sedilla collected some pebbles, Owen edged round the side. Above the cave, the cliffs of the Ridge rose sheer; but to one side of the entrance there was a small rock. Owen crept behind it. The plan worked well. Sedilla threw her pebbles hard against her side of the rock, then retreated fast. Immediately the two guards swung round and Owen slipped into the cave.

At first he could see nothing; but as his eyes grew accustomed to the dark, he noticed a red circle of light glowing dimly from the ground. Startled, he saw it was Cyclops, asleep with her eye open. How she had changed. She looked bedraggled and old. Her face was distorted; her arms and antennae were in disarray; her eye was dim and blurred.

Then Owen heard a moan from nearby, and looking round, caught a glint of silver from Faluffel's paper-clip where her feathery arms had been bound with her necklace. She was lying face down on the ground. Owen swam quietly to her and gently turned her over. She gasped when she saw who it was and whispered quickly, "Hurry, untie me. She's completely mad. She says she's going to kill me tomorrow if Charles doesn't take her back and dissolve our marriage."

Suddenly there was a stir, and Cyclops, who had been disturbed by the whispering, half sat up. Opening her mouth, she gave out a peal of laughter, then broke into song.

"Don't worry, she's still asleep. Just keep quiet for a while."

Sure enough, Cyclops lay back again and started snoring.

Owen knelt down, and by unbending the clip behind her back, was easily able to slip the string from between. She'd been cut by the end of the clip as she struggled to ease it around to the front without success, and there were bruises on her back.

"Please hurry," she whispered. "She won't sleep for much longer. Oh Owen, I'm so pleased to see you. How is Charles?"

"The Copepods set on him. He's alive but a bit battered. No, don't worry, he'll recover. The Great Pond Snail is looking after him. Rottifer and Ostracod are going to escort him to Bear's Bucket where you arranged to meet if anything went wrong. I ..."

Just then, the paper-clip slipped off the rock and clattered to the floor of the cave. At once Cyclops awoke and reared up. Her eye brightened and flashed wildly. Then she spotted Owen and screamed with rage.

"So, you've come to take her away, have you? We'll soon see about that."

Owen grabbed the clip. Its end was still opened up, and he clutched it hard as she came towards him. But the Cyclops looked so fearsome: her single eye glowered crimson, her great egg-sacs jolting against her sides, her purple arms bristling madly as she came leaping towards him. Owen cried out in terror. Dashing the paper-clip out of Owen's hands, the Cyclops made to hurl her full weight against him. Owen ducked out of her reach, then ran towards the cave entrance. "Hurry, Faluffel, follow me," he shouted.

But he'd scarcely reached the mouth of the cave before he heard a sob behind him. Faluffel had been caught and her two arms were already being tied together again with the paper-clip and string. At the same time, Owen saw Sedilla, swimming flat out towards him with the two fat guards in hot pursuit.

"Quick, Owen. Swim up the cliff face and onto the Ridge as fast as you can or we'll all be killed!"

"Faluffel, we'll get help straight away and be back to rescue you."

Owen joined Sedilla and they swam up, away from the guards. But they'd gone only a short distance when they heard a yell behind them. Cyclops had attacked one of the guards, giving him a vicious bite. He stumbled and fell, crying out with pain.

"How dare you leave your guard-post, you worthless 'thing'," she screeched, giving him a second bite. Then she turned to bite the second guard, but he'd disappeared into the cave, so she decided to chase Owen and Sedilla instead. Unfortunately the black shapes had been attracted by the noise, and soon it became imperative for all three to scramble up the cliff rather than swim.

Owen and Sedilla were pulling themselves onto a plateau just below the top of the Ridge when a very strange thing happened. Both Sedilla's feathery arms and Owen's hands were imprisoned by two enormous feet pressing down on them from the ledge above. They both squealed with shock. They were left dangling helplessly in the water.

"What's happening to us?" asked Owen. "Cyclops will get us if we don't free ourselves."

He tried to lean outwards but could see nothing.

"I don't know," squeaked Sedilla, frightened, "but whoever it is, they're deliberately exposing us to the full view of the Sticklebacks, and if they don't let us go soon, we'll be eaten."

"Quite so, quite so," said a horrible husky voice. "And that's precisely what I intend. I'm using you as bait."

"What do you mean? Who are you, and what do you want?" Owen asked angrily.

"I'm a Fluke, and my name is Diplozoon Paradoxum. I'm a paradox because I'm really two animals joined into one; and we have a foot each don't we dear? And we've grown together across the middle, haven't we dear?"

"Yes, that's right," said a higher female voice, "grown together, never to part. Tee hee hee hee."

"Well, will both of you untread us immediately," said Sedilla sharply. "I've heard of the Fluke and I know full well that Flukes like you don't eat water-fleas or Boy-animalcules."

"And you're perfectly right. I've no intention of eating you. Have we dearest?"

"No", said the other voice. "I can think of nothing more tedious than the thought of eating water-fleas or Boy-animalcules."

"Then what are you going to do with us? Please let us go. We're being chased by Cyclops."

But Cyclops had seen them caught by the Fluke and was doubled over with laughter.

"What a fine sight. What a pretty picture. Well done, Fluke. I'll leave them entirely in your capable feet. Oh ha ha ha."

She was about to turn and go down to her cave when she saw

the second Copepod swim frantically away, purple with rage and indignation.

"You witch, you've killed my friend. I'm leaving. None of us Copepods will ever help you again. We'll have Charles as our leader and Faluffel can escape as far as I'm concerned. You're mad and cruel. Goodbye."

"No, no! She mustn't escape," Cyclops yelled. "Charles shall never have her. I'll dispose of her first," and she scrambled down the cliff towards the cave.

"Oh poor Faluffel," wailed Sedilla. "However can we help her now?"

"How indeed?" said the Fluke, leaning over to leer at them.

The Fluke was the most disgusting thing Owen had ever set eyes on. He could hardly bear to look. There were certainly two bodies but they were like two wrinkled up old socks. At the bottom of their bodies they'd grown together and a knobbly knee supported each side.

The Sticklebacks were approaching and Owen cringed.

"Please let us go," he pleaded. "Can't you see the Sticklebacks coming?"

"Precisely so, and I'm using you exactly for that purpose. To attract the Sticklebacks here; right where I want them."

"But why do you want us for bait? I don't understand."

"Very simple," said the husky voice. "We've only a few hours left to live unless we can attach ourselves to a Stickleback. We are a parasite, you see, and the Stickleback is our host."

"Oh, how horrid," said Sedilla. "Then we shall die." And she started to cry.

"Look, Sedilla," said Owen suddenly. "Look, isn't that Faluffel?"

Sedilla looked down. There were two tiny figures walking out of the cave. She stared harder. Yes, it was Faluffel all right. She was being hauled away from the cave by Cyclops. Her arms were still tied behind her, fastened with the paper-clip Owen had failed to use in his cowardice, and she was being pulled along by the piece of string.

"Goodbye Faluffel," said Owen sadly as the tiny figures disappeared.

"Faluffel," screamed Sedilla. "We'll follow."

"No you won't," said the Fluke, laughing harshly.

Sedilla looked straight ahead and turned deathly pale, for there, swimming right at them, was a huge Stickleback, his eyes bulging and his gloating mouth wide open. He'd heard the scream, and saw the bait dangling in front of him like a gift.

"Stay near me, Owen, and we'll both be eaten together," said Sedilla.

The Stickleback was almost upon them; then there was a flash of silver, and just as the huge fish was about to eat them, the Fluke gave an almighty leap onto the fish's head. Quickly it glued its feet onto the fish's gills, and Owen and Sedilla were sent tumbling down through the water into a deep crevice.

The huge fish lurched about trying to get rid of its parasite which he would have to support from now on, but the Fluke wouldn't budge. Angrily the fish swam away.

*Owen could see the Hydra witch stuck to a fat branch
and, fortunately, immobile. Her tubular body,
like a shapeless sack, was a violent green.*

13

THE HYDRA WITCH

They had just decided that it was safe to come out of hiding, when they saw Daphnia and Bosmina climbing cautiously down the cliff towards the cave. They all hugged and greeted one another and began swopping their tales. Both were able at last to discuss with admiration Sedilla's 5p circle – a present from Owen which made them both more than a little envious. But Sedilla said urgently:

"There's no time to waste now; we must follow Faluffel immediately, before Cyclops 'disposes' of her. It will be easy for the four of us to overcome Cyclops."

They scrambled down the rest of the cliff to where the two tiny figures had disappeared.

Sedilla's heart sank. The path they had chosen would lead them into sheer desolation; down to the deepest part of the Pond. Already the vegetation was becoming sparse, and instead of living matter, debris and decaying Detritus formed a sticky layer of mud, so it was easier to swim low over the surface than to walk. Fanning out in a line where they could all see one another, they hurried through the gloom, their shadows swimming darkly underneath them.

Soon the lack of oxygen slowed them to a type of swimming that was more of a wading. It took all their energy to go a very short distance. When they arrived at a wide pit where yellow bubbles squeezed through the ooze, rather like a porridge bubbling in a pot, they stopped altogether. Sedilla backed away, startled.

"Take care. These bubbles are poisonous. Don't go too near. They're filled with sulphur dioxide, methane, carbon dioxide. To go into one will be instant death."

"It's true," said Daphnia. "We can't possibly carry on. I've heard of foul creatures living in this Profundal zone who try to persuade you to take a ride in such a bubble. When that bubble arrives at the surface and bursts, your dead body hurtles down again to the creature waiting below."

After hearing this story, none of them wanted to continue, and as the path divided at this place – due probably to other creatures making the same decision as themselves – the second path was chosen. Besides, this way led upwards out of the mud and murk.

"No-one in their right mind would continue past this point," said Bosmina.

"But you forget," said Sedilla, worried. "Cyclops is *not* in her right mind."

Soon, however, they were swimming up the second path. It seemed to run parallel to the large Ridge. On either side the rock sloped sheer into darkness below. Before long, cool currents from above allowed them to breathe more freely and they travelled faster. Visibility improved and vegetation took a hold, increasing to fill the whole Ridge as if desperate to find a place before the precipice dropped away. Eventually they reached a glade where the Sun struggled through, illuminating an avenue ahead. They all dropped into the glade and lay exhausted.

Sedilla was the first to raise her head and, spotting some succulent-looking Algae growing from the weeds, urged them to eat some of the long crispy strands to build up their energy. Daphnia showed Owen how to crack open the stalks and suck out the sweet juices.

Soon they were rested and ready to travel on. The avenue was beautiful to swim through, for the trunks that lined each side were rounded and massive and pushed so tightly together that they touched all the way up, forming a complete wall. Overhead, the frond-branches were closely interwoven, like a mat. Along this avenue Owen and the water-fleas swam. It was deliciously cool. They found it so satisfying and easy to go with the current that they were lulled into contentment.

Suddenly, a sharp arrow soared through the water over Bosmina's head, streaked past Owen's ear and thundered into the trunk behind. They shrieked as the trunk split itself open, spilling its green contents into the avenue. There was a rush in the water. Owen saw that Sedilla had turned sharply and was holding her feathery arms to shield the others.

"It's Hermione, the Hydra witch. Quick, go back. Swim as fast as you can. Stand clear of her arrows: they'll paralyse you."

Daphnia, who was last, had already started back, pushing hard against the whirling current. The others pressed themselves flat against the trunks. There was no escape above or to the side as the thick trees made an impenetrable barrier.

Owen turned to see if Sedilla was all right. She signalled that she was. Behind her, Owen could see the Hydra witch stuck to a fat branch and, fortunately, immobile. Her tubular body, like a shapeless sack, was a violent green. Out from her head a crown of ten long ropey tentacles swayed this way and that through the water, rippling with the current.

There was another whistling noise from behind as three more arrows shot past and struck the ceiling above their heads, tearing the fronds apart, filling the water with a strong acrid taste.

"Sedilla, are you there?" Owen cried over his shoulder as he swam.

The green liquid swirling round obscured his view, but he could see that the Hydra was extending her tentacles towards them like a giant octopus. He wished that Daphnia would hurry up in front.

"Yes, I'm following. I'm ..." But she never finished her sentence, for another two arrows whizzed by. One hurtled straight into her back. She uttered a small cry: "Owen ..." then fell silent. With her antennae hanging limply by her sides, her feet pointing downwards and her heart still, Sedilla sank to the Bottom.

Before the tentacles could reach her, Owen and Bosmina lifted her body and, carrying it between them, swam backwards through the current until they were safely into the glade. There they laid their bundle gently down on the moss.

For a long time no-one said anything. Bosmina's face was hard and unflinching: Owen's white and drawn. Then Daphnia started sobbing uncontrollably. After a while she stopped. All three stared at Sedilla pondering her death. There they sat, huddled and silent. At last, Bosmina spoke.

"We must go on. Carry on without her."

"Yes, we must be brave," added Daphnia. Composing herself with great effort, she turned to Bosmina.

"You have to lead us from now on. Are you ready?"

Bosmina nodded and touched Daphnia's feathery arm as a sign of acceptance. She was now in control of her emotions. She had never really lost control. Owen still stared down. He felt as though his heart had died with Sedilla.

The water-fleas had nearly accepted Sedilla's death. She would become part of the Detritus. Only her memory would remain. Someone to think of when they needed strength.

Then all at once, something happened to Owen. What was wrong with them all? Didn't they realise that Sedilla, his Sedilla, the one he loved most in all the world, was dead?

Angrily he turned from Bosmina to Daphnia, wading over to the avenue entrance. He stared along its tunnelled opening, his fury bubbling up from deep inside. The avenue was no longer beautiful. It was hateful, full of malice. Pond-life too, he realised, was treacherous and cruel. One creature could poison another, tear them in two, and worse. Then his anger turned in upon himself. Why hadn't he protected Sedilla? She must have realised the full extent of the danger they would be facing to save Faluffel. All he had done was to get lost and then be too cowardly to kill Cyclops.

He stood there for a long time. The current whipped sharply at his back, and the salt welling out of his eyes stung and pricked them. Slowly other feelings took over from anger. Feelings of love and tenderness. Then a strange sensation came over him, almost as though someone was calling.

Suddenly Owen was swimming back to the body. He bent over it looking so wild and terrible that Daphnia and Bosmina stood aghast. Gripping Sedilla by the shoulders, Owen started to shake her; gently at first, then urgently.

"Sedilla, wake up. It's me, Owen. Wake up! Wake up!"

Bosmina and Daphnia looked at him astonished; as if he had gone mad. Then a glance of pity passed between them. He had not yet learned. Death was a natural part of Pond-life. Sedilla was now just an empty shell. Already they were thinking of the future, discussing plans. But Owen gathered Sedilla in his arms and gently rocked her to and fro. He must try to get her circulation going.

"Wake up, Sedilla. It's me, Owen. Please wake up!"

But the only sound was the rush of water from behind him as an enormous brown beetle charged down like a torpedo boat, landing a little way off. On his rowing legs were long hairy fringes and underneath his abdomen a bubble of air glinted like quicksilver.

Owen hardly noticed his presence. He didn't particularly mind whether he was eaten or not; but Daphnia gave a shriek of welcome.

"It's Geoffroy; Corixa Geoffroyi, the Lesser Water Boatman. Come and help us!"

The beetle stirred and looked round, then, recognising Daphnia, swam slowly over.

"What's the matter?" he enquired.

"Everything," Daphnia sobbed. "Sedilla's dead; killed by the Hydra witch; Faluffel can't be found, and now we have to persuade Owen to return with us."

"Return?" said Owen, shaken. "I can't leave her. There's something about her. Something not quite dead. Oh, I don't know." He hid his face in his hands.

"Hmm. I can see you're muddled and confused," said Geoffroy. He wandered over to Sedilla and looked closely at her. Then he passed his sensitive leg hairs gently over her face and looked closely into her heart.

"Hmm. I can see what you mean. Maybe she is ... no, I'm afraid she isn't." He stood for a moment in thought; then suddenly he said: "Goodness me, my air-supply is running out. It's always doing that. I'll give your problem some consideration while I'm away. Then I'll be back," and he rushed up out of sight.

Bosmina approached Owen. "You must accept these things as part of Pond-life. Learn to ponder and accept. Come back with us now." Her voice was full of wisdom and experience. Looking up at her, Owen agreed to return. But he could no longer bear to look at Sedilla.

"You see, above the Green, we bury our dead first, before we leave them."

"But there is really no need here," said Daphnia. "Everything will work out. You'll see. We'll look after you."

There was another rush of water and the Boatman was with them again.

"I'm afraid I can't think of a solution," he said sadly, looking defeated.

"It's all right," Daphnia explained. "He's coming with us. We'll go on to Bear's Bucket and tell the others. We'll take the way we came, unless this path leads on to the Ridge."

"No, it doesn't. It ends just below the surface where the Rat-tailed Maggot lives. Then there's nothing between it and the Ridge except a deep drop down to the Valley of Death ... wait a minute. I've just thought of something. The Rat-tailed Maggot is a healer, he might help. But how to get there past the Hydra. Hmm. Hmm." Here the Boatman began to row himself in circles. This helped to clear his brain.

"Ahh," he continued. "You're not afraid, are you?" he said to Owen.

"No, not any more. What must I do?"

"You can climb upon my back. No, that won't work. Too slippery. Hmm." Geoffroy started to row back the other way. "Aah, that's it. You can travel in my air-bubble. Come on."

And Owen was not afraid. He would never be a coward again. He said goodbye, telling them he'd meet them at Bear's Bucket if he could find it. Gathering Sedilla's body under him, with one arm holding her tight, he ran up to the great beetle, dived headlong through into the bubble, and they were off.

Owen stood with Sedilla in his arms and regarded the Maggot
with great attention. He was not afraid, although
the Maggot was very large indeed.

14

THE RAT-TAILED MAGGOT

Owen was rowed through the water in great sweeping arcs. He could see nothing through the bubble except streaks of light; but holding Sedilla made him feel safe. He let the sensation of going along fill his whole body. He wished it would go on forever. But it was over in a moment, for the Boatman had landed at the far end of the path, just below the surface.

Owen dived out with his precious bundle, landing on the silt. The green light was so intense that he was unable to see for a few seconds, but when he could, he saw that he was in a strange land composed entirely of sandy mounds. Such a strong current passed over them, it was like standing on a mountain-top in a high wind. The green light was darker than the green of the Centre, and Owen noticed that it was coming from plants with leaves shaped like water-lilies. Under each plant, a thick bunch of roots hung white and wriggling in the current, casting shadows on the mound like balls of tangled string.

"Don't worry about the current," said Geoffroy. "It comes from water entering the Pond. You'll get used to it." He began to look anxiously at his air-bubble again and, realising his impatience to be off, Owen thanked him kindly for his help.

"Well," said Geoffroy. "The Rat-tailed Maggot, the Pond-phenomenon, the Speciality of the Shallows, is just over there. You can't miss him. Goodbye, and good luck." And the great beetle took off straight over the precipice, plunged down low for a while like a heavy sea-plane, then arc-ed straight up to the surface. Owen walked to the very end of the path. He could see no-one.

Imagine Owen's surprise when he found that the Rat-tailed Maggot had been there all the time. He was so vast and so white and so lined that the shadows of wrinkled string from the roots above camouflaged him perfectly.

Owen stood with Sedilla in his arms and regarded the Maggot with great attention. He was not afraid, although the Maggot was very large indeed.

You don't look like a rat or a maggot, he thought. You don't even have a tail. But what you do look like is an elephant; a Pond-elephant. You're as big as one, and have a long wrinkled trunk that stretches up right to the water-skin and may even go through it. Your legs, though shorter and stumpier, are definitely elephant's legs; you have an ear-trumpet on this side, and there may be one on the other if I walk around. You have two tusk-like things below the trumpets, and even your skin is thick, rough and wrinkly like an elephant's ... in a kind of dirty white. That's what you are, a white elephant, only you're back to front; your trunk has been put on where your tail should be.

Then Owen remembered that none of the Pond-creatures would have seen a real elephant, so how could they know he'd been given the wrong name?

Owen had now completely confused himself over which end to address, so he compromised and laid the bundle gently down half-way between each end. But the Rat-tailed Maggot had been fully aware of Owen's presence from the start, and the end opposite to the trunk turned slowly round to look at him. He had the gentlest eyes Owen had ever seen. They twinkled benignly from a forest of little creases and, on seeing Sedilla, were immediately filled with sorrow.

"Turn her over so that she is heart-side up, and I will take a sounding," he said in a voice so mellow that Owen felt hopeful again.

Very gently, the Pond-elephant lowered his trunk, shortening it as though he was shutting a telescope. Then he swung it round and extended it until the very tip touched Sedilla's heart. He listened intently, and Owen saw his eyes roll up as he pondered.

The suspense was terrible. Owen's stomach turned over and over. After a few seconds which seemed like an eternity, the eyes rolled down and the Pond-elephant spoke.

"There's a faint flutter, a slight whisper, a small murmur; but there's only one way to find out."

So saying, the Pond-elephant curled his trunk round Sedilla, Lifted her bodily, and swung her rapidly round. Then he replaced her carefully where she had lain before. Sedilla had gone a pale rose-colour all over. But even as they watched, the colour faded and went back to white.

"How did she die?" the Pond-elephant enquired. "This is an important point for a healer such as myself to know."

"The Hydra shot her with an arrow."

"But that's impossible. Why the whisper if she's dead? No-one escapes the Hydra's arrow and lives. I don't understand. Don't understand at all."

Then poor Faluffel and Cyclops must have died too, Owen thought. They couldn't possibly have escaped the Hydra. He started to cry.

The Pond-elephant was so distressed by Owen crying at what he thought was his failure to revive Sedilla, that he lowered his trunk again, listened, nodded his head, picked her up and shook her as hard as he could, grunting and trumpeting like an elephant.

All at once, Sedilla went bright purple and squeaked.

Owen jumped up and down with delight, and the Pond-creature moved his feet (which is a very rare thing for a Rat-tailed Maggot to do – normally he likes to keep perfectly still). Then he grew puzzled and turned Sedilla over. The silver circle. Whatever was it? But before he had time to ask, Sedilla tried to speak. First there was a small flutter from one of her arms, then her mouth opened and began to move, and a far-away voice muttered something as if in a trance.

"My silver 5p ... my silver 5p ..." it murmured.

"Sedilla, you're alive!" cried Owen. "You're going to be all right."

Sedilla opened her eyes, and gradually the shine came back into them. She moved her arms, then gulped in some water and rested a while. As her circulation began to move of its own accord, she raised herself a little and smiled at Owen and the Rat-tailed Maggot.

"It was my silver 5p, my silver 5p that saved me."

"What, the silver circle? How?" asked the Maggot in wonder.

They both bent over her and listened carefully.

"The arrow," she said quietly. "The arrow bounced off the 5p before much of the poison could come in. I feel stunned; in a sort of trance, but I'm not paralysed at all."

Owen was amazed. He inspected the place where the arrow had entered. There, sure enough, was a hole. Peering closer, he saw on the 5p piece, right on Her Majesty's ear, a small nick where the arrow had struck.

Owen had never felt so happy in is life. Sedilla staggered to her feet, hugged Owen and stroked the Pond-elephant's trunk.

Then the Maggot made Sedilla walk round so her circulation would keep going, and Owen told her all that had happened. Sedilla cried when she heard about Faluffel and started to turn pale. The Pond-elephant grew alarmed, took another sounding and made her walk about again. This time, Sedilla told Owen about the Hydra.

"Water-fleas are her favourite diet. She searches for them with her long tentacles and her appetite is almost insatiable. Sometimes she eats so much that she expands and produces daughter-buds from her side. These get so greedy that they even fight with their own mother to get food, which is ridiculous really because they all own the same stomach."

"What a foul creature," said Owen. "But what did it feel like when the arrow got you? Was it very painful?"

"No, I felt nothing. The effect was instantaneous. She's a clever old witch, Hermione the Hydra. I'll tell you how the arrows work. At the end of each tentacle there's a swollen lump. Inside each lump is a cnidoblast. When the Hydra fires this, it uncurls a long hollow rope with a harpoon-headed arrow on the end. This sticks into her prey and up the hollow coiled rope she sends poison which paralyses her 'food' so that she can draw it into her body with her tentacles."

"Then it should be impossible to escape Hydra?"

"Yes, Heliozoa's spicule would have been useless, too. It's pointless slashing bits off her or her daughter-buds; they just grow all over again ... so do the slashed-off pieces. They say that even if you turn her inside out, the cells merely swop positions as if nothing had happened."

But Owen didn't want to hear anything more about the Hydra and as Sedilla felt nearly well they went back to get another sounding.

"One more walk round and she'll be fine," the healer promised.

Owen decided to tell Sedilla that the Rat-tailed Maggot was really an elephant. As he described the elephant he bent down and very carefully drew one for her. But it didn't work because Sedilla just said: "What a beautiful drawing of the Rat-tailed Maggot, except that you've got him back to front and the breathing-tube is on his face. But do show it to the Rat-tailed Maggot before the current sweeps it away." So Owen gave up. Some things were just too difficult to explain, and as Sedilla's final sounding was satisfactory, they asked if they could go.

"I'm afraid you cannot go," said the Maggot sadly. "There's no way back past the Hydra, unless the Boatman calls for you again."

"But we have to get to Bear's Bucket to let the others know we're safe."

"If you go down that path, before you even get to the Hydra, there's Glossosiphonia Complanata, the disagreable leech. He is an enormous rubbery thing with concentric rings around the body that can make it squidge any way he wants. If you walk across his land he will jump onto your head and fix himself on with his sucker at the end of his body. He makes awful sucking noises as he devours your juices. He'll never let you pass by."

"Then I don't want to go that way at all," said Sedilla, "and the very thought of meeting the Hydra once more makes me feel quite pale."

Sure enough, Sedilla had grown strangely white, and the Maggot had to give her a small shake.

"Then we shan't," Owen announced. "Can't we go over the edge of the precipice, then down across the Bottom and up onto the Ridge again?"

"Yes, on the Bottom is only a tiny valley with the Ridge and the safety of the Shallows beyond; but it's the deepest part of the Pond – the Valley of Death. It is guarded by Dugesia Lugubris and his gang. They'll never let you through. No-one has ever reached the other side. All around the valley sweeps the Edge, rising steeply to the surface, pockmarked with the holes of the Furry Monsters, and above is the favourite haunt of the black shapes."

"I've heard of the flat worm, Dugesia Lugubris," Sedilla spoke slowly and heavily. "He is the most treacherous creature in the whole Pond. Yet that is the way we'll have to go."

"Then may our Sun-god's light go with you, for you'll need it," said the Maggot, seeing that their minds were made up. "Go down under the swirling current. That will protect you for at least part of the way."

As they walked to the edge of the precipice, Owen and Sedilla heard a great sigh escaping from the Rat-tailed Maggot. He looked sad as they turned to wave, but gave a slight inclination of his head. He had fixed himself back in his original position and stood perfectly still. He felt very alone. Not many people came his way. They all got eaten before they arrived. How sad that those he had so recently helped would surely perish in the Valley of Death. Pond-life, he thought, was very complex.

*As Owen and Sedilla approached, they stood
upright and still, facing them straight on, daring
them to advance across their plain.*

15

THE POND-GHOSTS

The current ran strongly above them, pressing with all its weight as they lowered themselves carefully over the precipice.

"Hold on tight," shouted Sedilla over the noise, "or we'll be dashed to pieces on the rocks below."

Owen travelled in front to catch Sedilla in case she fell. It was just like being beneath a waterfall with such a thunderous current. There was nothing to see but violent streaks of white, silver and grey.

Clutching at the rocks, they climbed slowly down, until eventually the current weakened. Then quite suddenly it subsided and they were in total calm. Above they could see it streaking away over the Valley to the Edge and the Shallows beyond. Below was stillness and silence. But now they had become aware of stray whirlpools spinning down like funnels, warning that Furry Monsters were around.

For a while they eased, crept and slid their way downwards, keeping to the shadow of the rocks, until Sedilla grew so pale that Owen had to stop and shake her hard to keep her circulation going.

The wedge of blackness that hung above the Valley below made their hearts sink. It lay like a piece of forgotten shadow over the Valley floor. It wasn't a very long wedge to cross; they could see the Ridge on the other side; nor was it deep; but above the wedge silent shoals of Sticklebacks darted this way and that. With their sharply-pointed fins projecting from their backs, they looked for all the world like huge black sharks.

Without further hesitation, Owen and Sedilla slid down the rest of the slope, then slipped straight through into the protection of the black shadow.

The dark closed about them, enveloping them in its cold embrace like a blanket of fog. They felt the foul stench, the rot and stagnation of the Profundal zone. It was a sour unwholesome odour, stifling and heavy. The mud was slimy underfoot and oozed through their toes as they waded along, but they dared not swim. They could hardly see through the dense atmosphere.

They had not taken more than twenty paces when they were confronted by a dreadful spectacle. The middle of the Valley was pitch black except for the smallest amount of light that penetrated the gloom in a series of thin shafts, which moved about illuminating the ground in circles. In this meagre light, they saw that the Bottom all around was infested with Planarian worms. It was Dugesia and his enormous flat-worm friends. They had been guarding their eggs; some in round black pods, others in pods which had stalks.

Already they had detected Owen and Sedilla from some distance away by using their sensory cells on their heads. As Owen and Sedilla approached, they stood upright and still, facing them straight on, daring them to advance across their plain.

"Well, Owen," said Sedilla in a hollow voice, "it's either death by these or the shapes above. Which shall it be?"

"But they don't look real," said Owen. "They can't be alive. That one, their leader, if it is Dugesia Lugubris, looks like a ghost. He's pitch black except for white circles around his eyes, and he's flat and ghostly in shape. Is he a Pond-ghost?"

"I don't know what you mean by 'ghost'. These are Planarian worms, renowned for their evil ways. They're so thin and flat that they can glide smoothly over the Bottom on a layer of slime they secrete. When they detect you they dash after you with amazing speed, throw themselves upon you and roll you flat."

"And then what?" Owen asked, his eyes wide with fright, his voice wobbling with fear.

"They wait, pressing down until you stop struggling. Then out of their middles comes a tube which is their mouth. This sticks into you and either cuts you up into little pieces small enough to be swallowed together with your juices, or sucks you completely dry. One minute you are full, the next, empty; and without your body juices you become quite insubstantial as you can well imagine."

"Yes," replied Owen. "It sounds ghastly."

"Well I'd rather be sucked dry than eaten by a Stickleback. That large mouth coming towards us under the feet of the Fluke was an experience not to be repeated."

"And we've nothing to defend ourselves with now, have we?"

"No. Heliozoa's spicule was left behind when the arrow pierced my shell." Said Sedilla, dejectedly. "But even if we could slash at them, unfortunately Planarian worms don't mind at all. Each piece just grows again. In fact, if they feel there are not enough of them, the wretched creatures can divide by tearing themselves across the middle in a kind of tug-of-war. The two pieces left then become new Planarian worms."

Owen looked around. Several 'crusts' lay about: empty cases and hollow creatures – all that remained of former victims of Dugesia Lugubris and his gang.

He stared at the black spectral creatures ahead waiting patiently in a line for their victims to cross their land. Sedilla smiled sadly and stroked his head tenderly with her feathery arm. She felt weak and tired.

"We must be courageous and at least try to swim across. The

distance is so short between here and the brown cliff. But can't you, Boy-Sapiens, think of any wise plan to outwit them? Ponder, Owen, ponder hard."

Owen looked at the crusts, then at the dreadful pods on their stalks. He watched the circles of light move mysteriously this way and that among them. Then to his alarm he glimpsed two other small creatures who had wandered into the same black shadow-land from further along on their side, not realising the danger ahead. The Pond-ghosts had already turned round and were detecting them.

"Oh, look!" said Owen, amazed. "When they turn round, the Pond-ghosts are so flat that they look like sticks."

"So they do," said Sedilla, "and quite unterrifying too. That's all those other poor creatures would have seen as they stepped unknowingly into the blackness. No wonder they didn't sense any danger. Oh no. I can't bear it," she covered her eyes with her arms. "I think they're both water-fleas."

Half the gang of Planarian worms had already thrown themselves flat on the ground, speeding up their sliding movements with muscular spasms in a race to slide there first over their own slime, then stand in a line to confront them, daring the new-comers to cross their land. It was horrible. Owen put his arms round Sedilla, partly to comfort her and partly for fear of losing her in the pitch black.

Suddenly he had an idea. "Sedilla, I've just noticed something. Look! When those circles of light come near the Pond-ghosts, they back away and try to avoid them. Don't you see, if we can get into a circle of light each and follow it wherever it goes, we could eventually get across without them daring to come near us."

"What a brilliant idea!" cried Sedilla. And she stopped shivering immediately and jumped into the very next circle of light that came along. Owen ran further along the bank before he could jump across into a circle of his own, but once inside, he could see the 5p in Sedilla's pouch glinting brightly from hers, confusing the Pond-ghosts who could detect her presence, but were repelled by the light and the additional flashing of her silver circle. Owen had nothing silvery to give him additional protection, for like a coward, he'd allowed the unbent paper-clip to be dashed all too easily from his hands inside Cyclops' cave.

He watched Sedilla gliding along ahead in her pool of brightness as if she were dancing with a mysterious partner who led her wherever he wanted to go. And while he was still sliding around in his circle, Sedilla's had already travelled towards the brown cliff, allowing her to make a terrific leap from her circle to another even nearer. All at once she disappeared. She was safely on the other side of the wedge.

Owen was still skating all over the black place in his circle, mostly in the wrong direction, and sometimes nearly back to the place they'd started from.

Then a scream of terror made him turn sharply. Dugesia and some of his gang had reached the two poor fleas further along. Owen stared hard at the two helpless creatures, then heard himself cry out. He'd caught sight of a shining paper-clip on one of the water-fleas – the one that was still held captive by the other – the Cyclops.

"Faluffel!" he screamed. "The circles of light! Use the circles of light!"

Both creatures understood immediately – but it was the Cyclops who pushed aside her prisoner with bristling arms and, giving a peal of demented laughter, leapt into the very next circle that came by and was soon waltzing away wherever it led, leaving poor Faluffel to her fate, in full view of the vile Planarians, who had now arrived.

And there was no circle of light coming her way.

But Faluffel wasn't eaten. She'd turned her back on the terrible sight to curl over herself and wait for her death.

... then she glanced around to find out why she wasn't being eaten, and noticed that it was the flashes of light reflecting off her silver paper-clip tying her arms together behind her back that made the worms recoil, and she was able to wait in that position until at last a circle of light came her way and she could do a gigantic flea-hop into it and skate quickly away.

Poor Owen found he was still travelling all over the place in his circle. Oh why wouldn't his pool of light carry him to safety? He seemed compelled for ever to dance round the dreadful pods. And now he saw the Planarians had decided to surround the two circles without the addition of any glinting silver – those of the Cyclops and himself.

Just then there was a loud 'crack' right next to him. One of the horrid pods burst open, spilling out a host of baby spectres. And there seemed to be no larval stage; the little ghosts were replicas of their parents, only smaller, and they were already looking out hungrily for a meal. It was worse than a nightmare.

"Owen!" shouted a voice quite near. And here was Faluffel inside her circle of light coming along right behind him. She had seen his predicament and signalled that she was about to make a clever flea-hop right into his circle.

Owen caught her and held her tight, lifting the paper-clip behind her back to gleam for them both as he danced her along.

But now, a series of the tiny Pond-ghosts began nibbling bites out of the end of Faluffel's necklace string which was left trailing outside their pool of light. Holding on to it with their little mouths, they were endeavouring to jerk the two dancers away from their light-pool. Owen frantically held Faluffel close with one arm while he tugged back the string with the other. Luckily, the string was now well-oiled from its slippery trailing through the slime, and soon wrenched from the tiny flat-worms' grasp, safely coiled in by Owen around his arm.

Their pool of light was unfortunately making its way straight towards the other flea now, and Owen could see illuminated inside her circle of light, a small wizened Cyclops, hardly recognizable. Her eye had dimmed to half its former glow. Her legs and arms were twisted and bent; her skin cracked and gnarled. But she had seen the trick of the glinting silver paper-clip and tried to intensify her own large single eye to make it glow stronger. But it had faded too far in her madness, and wasn't bright enough to keep the worms away. For the whole of Dugesia's gang now surrounded her, waiting for an opportunity to attack.

Cyclops saw that the nearest circle was one which had Owen and Faluffel in it just behind her. Without more ado, she hurtled madly towards them in an ungainly leap, meaning to push Owen from his circle and let him perish, while grabbing Faluffel and her paper-clip to keep herself safe. But her leap was not strong enough and Dugesia was ready to waylay her. He stood up to intercept her clumsy attempt, flinging his slimy body on top of hers, flattening her into the mud. In vain Cyclops struggled and in vain tried to flash her eye in order to ward him off. But the eye remained dim and powerless. She gave a final scream of rage as Dugesia inserted his sucking-beak and began to withdraw her juices. Owen saw her quiver and die, then had to turn away. Soon she would be a dry crust lying forever in the Valley of Death.

Their circle had moved away again, but then he saw his chance. Several shafts of light were travelling towards the brown cliff. Owen jumped through the water to the safety of the first; bounded easily into the second, then the third as they almost touched in passing.

He was through the Valley of Death and could pull Faluffel by her string up on to the safety of the brown cliff. Some little distance away, he saw Sedilla cowering behind a rock. She had heard the screams and thought Owen had been caught.

"You've made it! You've made it!" she exclaimed, coming towards him.

"And so have I," squeaked another flea who had collapsed exhausted onto the ground behind him. Sedilla stared in amazement. It was Faluffel.

*They all grew quiet, and out of the Bucket walked a tiny Bear;
a very small but dignified Bear. Without bothering to look
left or right at his audience, he plodded purposefully towards his food.*

16

BEAR'S BUCKET

Sunlight, yellow and bright, flooded the water with such richness and profusion that Faluffel and Sedilla's eyes shone with happiness. It shimmered on the mudflats that spread in uneven ripples on all sides, dappling them with patterns of lacy light. Among the mudflats, shingle and sand had been formed into ridges by small waves. These lapped gently at the shore, slapping against the stones and swaying the water-reeds and rushes which were growing abundant and green. Beyond the water-skin they could see the shadows of colossal buds packed tight with petals waiting to unfold. The water was warm and restful, perfumed with fresh plant smells. The three creatures felt that all the worms, creepy crawlies, the darkness and cold, the fear and unhappiness were just a forgotten nightmare. They had journeyed up the brown cliff from the wedge to the Shallows, laughing and crying alternately. Here, with all stories told and everybody safe, it was a paradise of comfort and peace.

"What a relief to be in the Littoral zone at last," sighed Sedilla. "The Shallows are so shiny and yellow without the blanket of Algae above, so bright I can't find what I'm looking for."

"What are you looking for?" Owen asked.

"The Bucket, of course. Bear's Bucket. It's a very large rusty Bucket – you can't miss it, they say. It marks the boundary of safety where creatures can assemble before facing the dangers of the Edge on the other side of the Shallows. We'll soon be there."

"I'm so longing to see Charles again," said Faluffel. "Poor Charles; he'll be so terribly wounded, but I'll love him all the more."

"And won't Daphnia and Bosmina be surprised to see you," said Owen to Sedilla.

"Owen, you must promise me not to be angry with them," said Sedilla, sternly. "How can they be expected to understand my revival? How wonderful it will be to be together again."

Owen promised. He had lost his anger anyway. He was so happy to have Sedilla back.

Cooler currents made the water quiver as they swam across the Shallows. The Sun, shining through, wobbled lazy patterns over their bodies and over the ground. They travelled through groves of dark green Duckweed, round stems of fat rushes and through clouds of sparkling bubbles which scattered as they passed, enriching the water with goodness.

"There it is!" shouted Faluffel excitedly.

The Bucket was just ahead, settled at the bottom of a shallow slope by a thick bank of reeds. In front of the Bucket was a grove of Pond-weed spaced carefully like an orchard. From the branches of these trees, strands of healthy-looking Algae hung intertwined like bunches of mistletoe. Green sponges covered some rotting wood that had fallen to one side of the Bucket. All the way round the rest of it in a kind of semi-circle, was a large mound of mud, positioned as if on purpose for all the creatures who gathered to watch Pond Bears from a 'safe' distance. There seemed to be quite a number at the moment, sitting in rows along the top of the mound.

As they approached the Bucket, Owen could see that it was a very ancient rusty child's seaside bucket which could have been there for years. It had fallen on its side and stuck, making a vast enclosure where creatures of all kinds could obtain good hiding places. It looked like a giant fortress, for there were numerous holes where cannons might have poked their way through. In many places round the rim, pieces had curled back and rusted away, leaving jagged structures like the crenellations on a castle wall.

Then they spotted Daphnia sitting lower down on her mound. Between Rottifer and Ostracod was Charles, looking huddled and drawn. As a bunch of Pond-creatures, there couldn't have been a more dejected and sorry-looking collection – especially when compared with the other excited creatures waiting to see the Bear.

When Charles heard the whoop of delight behind him, he turned and jumped up as though he had been stung by a sponge-spicule.

"My Faluffel, my Faluffel, you're saved!" he shouted, rushing down from the mound; and although several of his arms were still not working, he hugged her tightly. Then he stared at Sedilla in disbelief. Behind him the others, especially Daphnia and Bosmina, stood amazed at the apparition of Sedilla, alive and well.

The greetings and hugging, with all its squeaking, grinning, blurps and dances, lasted for quite a while. When everyone tried to tell their stories at once, they were all thoroughly confused. Eventually they ended up listening to Faluffel's story: it was incredible …

"After you saw me being tied up and led away by Cyclops," she began, "she took me down a terrifying path. It seemed to get lower and lower and darker and darker. She wouldn't let me take the upper path, but made me go straight past the evil-smelling bubbles. They were vile. She said she was going to feed me to the nastiest member of the Pond, but when I suggested that the nastiest member of the Pond might eat her as well, she retorted that the light from her eye would protect her. That's why, Owen, I understood so quickly the value of the circles of light."

"What circles of light? They sound magical to me," said Charles.

"Our Sun-god sent circles of light to get us across Dugesia's Valley of Death. We all escaped except Cyclops, who was killed by Dugesia himself. She was sucked dry. She will be a crust forever," said Sedilla.

"What a relief," they all said.

"Owen, it was your wonderful clever things from above the Green; the silver 5p and paper-clip, that saved us" said Faluffel.

They all clapped and cried "Hurrah", until Owen went pink with embarrassment and tried to change the subject. "Charles, are you recovering well?"

"I'm completely well again now I've got Faluffel," he said tenderly. But Charles did look a little strange. His antennae were still wrinkled, and he tried to cover up his wounds with his arms. Owen thought his injuries added a certain heroic air to his character so that he looked like a wounded soldier back from the wars.

"And we got here safely," Charles continued, "except for one little incident with the Rotifer."

"Oh do tell us," pleaded Daphnia.

"He got all wound up by Gordius the Nematode worm. Gordius was so long you couldn't see the other end. Ostracod grabbed the top end of the worm and I grabbed the bottom and we managed to unwind him till the Rotifer could gyrate himself free."

"Grrr," said Ostracod, "and we coiled Gordius round a weed-stem and tied the end together in a knot to serve him right."

This time it was Rottifer who grew embarrassed, so he suggested they go to watch the Bear. They walked over and sat with the other creatures to wait.

"You see, the Pond Bear only comes when he wants to, grrr. He's bound to sooner or later," explained Ostracod.

"He just loves to, blurp, keep other people waiting. Blurp.blurp,

blurp," said Rottifer.

"But I didn't know that Ponds had Bears," said Owen.

"And why should they not have Bears?" said Sedilla. "This Pond Bear is a highly respected Pond Bear. He lives in a Bucket which he calls his cave. We all love him, and his name is Sigismund Tardigrada."

"But isn't he a Furry Monster? Bears are, above the Green. And won't he eat you?"

"Oh no," said Bosmina. "He's a very friendly Bear, and he only eats plants, because that's what Pond Bears eat."

"He has a whole forest of Algae growing just outside his Bucket," said Daphnia, "so he doesn't have to walk very far. He is very slow and only ambles along. That's why he's called Tardigrada, or 'slow-walker.'"

"And as for being a Furry Monster," laughed Sedilla, "he isn't a Furry Monster, he's a Bear-animalcule and he hasn't any fur at all."

"He's entirely a bare Bear," sniggered Bosmina.

"A naked Bear," giggled Faluffel.

"A transparent Bear," growled Ostracod.

"A harmless, hairless Bear, blurp, blurp, blurp," said Rottifer.

"How very strange. I can hardly picture him," said Owen. "Doesn't he mind you all watching like this?"

"Well he does and he doesn't," said Charles. "Half of him is very proud of being the most impressive member of the Pond, yet the other part of him wants to be fierce and frighten people away. That's why he's chosen this Bucket to live in, because when he growls, his minute growl will echo against the metal sides and become A VERY LARGE GROWL to frighten people away."

"It's perfectly true," squeaked Faluffel, "except that he doesn't scare people. Pond Bears, you know, shed their skin at intervals when they want to get bigger. This Pond Bear has nailed up a former skin of his own, or one of his fore-bears, onto a post, to warn people off. But you can hardly see it's there because it's transparent. You can only see his claws, his eyes, his nose and his outline."

"And it doesn't scare anyone away as it's meant to," said Bosmina. "Look, it's just over there." She pointed to a board, which had a skin stretched over it.

Owen stared fixedly at the fore-bear. He wasn't frightened of it either. It definitely didn't have any fur ... but there was something else about it that was different from a Bear above the Green.

Just then, there was a kind of snuffling noise, followed by a small grunt, followed almost immediately by a LARGE GRUNT that echoed deeply in the interior of the Bucket.

"Sshh!" said Sedilla, "he's coming out."

They all grew quiet, and out of the Bucket walked a tiny Bear; a very small but dignified Bear. Without bothering to look left or right at his audience, he plodded purposefully towards his food. Owen watched intently. He was thrilled. It was a real Bear after all. And then he noticed the difference.

"Sedilla," he whispered. "That's not very big for a Bear to be, but I've just noticed what's wrong with him. He's got more legs than an ordinary Bear."

"Well, why shouldn't he if he wants to?" said Sedilla, sounding annoyed. "Surely he has the right to have as many legs as he wants, and I don't see what's wrong about it."

Owen felt ashamed. Why should Bears above the Green be right and Pond Bears be wrong? Who was he to say what was right or wrong? Anyway, the Pond Bear could have evolved before the Land Bear for all he knew.

"I'm sorry," he apologised, "I do like the Pond Bear very much. Thank you for showing him to me."

The Pond Bear had reached the nearest Algae plant, and although it looked fairly eaten already, he climbed the stalk, holding on with his claws, and started to eat. Then another Bear followed him out of the Bucket, climbed the stalk and also began to eat.

"That's a female Bear-animalcule!" said Bosmina. "He's found a mate at last! How very thrilling."

Then more Pond Bears appeared and started to play together.

"Oh, little Bears!" said Daphnia. "How charming. I'm so very pleased they've had a family. Such adorable little creatures."

Everyone said "Ahh, aren't they sweet!" And "Oohh, the dear little cubs," and other such appropriate comments, as they sat and watched.

"Clever these Pond Bears," growled Ostracod, "and you know why? Because they have a brain. Only a small one, mind you, but it's there, grrrr. Look, you can see it faintly outlined on the skin."

He nodded towards the fore-bear on the post. By screwing up his eyes and staring hard, Owen agreed he could make out a faint shadow.

"Yes, grrr. And when – or rather if – the Pond dries up ..." here everyone shifted uncomfortably. They didn't like to hear about such possibilities ... "Pond Bears are able to contract into a *dormant* form of Bear. This is called a Bear Barrel. In this state, they are able to withstand fantastic drought until the Pond returns to normal."

"And it only takes an hour for him to change back into a Pond Bear again," said Sedilla.

"That's very clever," Owen agreed. He wondered what a Bear Barrel would look like.

"Oh do tell him about the Museum, blurp, blurp," pleaded Rottifer.

"Oh yes, do tell him," Sedilla encouraged him. Aside to Owen she whispered, "Ostracod is very impressed by Pond Bears, you know. They are his favourite subject. He can go on about them for ages."

"Well, grrr, it is passed down, grr, and all perfectly true, grrr, that a Pond Bear was once stored on some hay as a Bear Barrel in a Museum for over a hundred years. And when they put this hay into some water, grr, grr, the Barrel emerged once more as a Pond Bear without any ill effect at all, grrr. It is the greatest example of prolonged drying for a Pond-creature that has ever been recorded."

"Wow! How amazing to be dried up for a hundred years then come back to life," exclaimed Owen.

"And what exactly is a Museum?" asked Faluffel, rather timidly.

"Growly wowly wowly grr," was all that Ostracod could say, and Charles, thinking this question too difficult for anyone to answer, told them all they were invited to accompany him and Faluffel up to the Spawn to see them off on their honeymoon.

As they approached, the milky film they had seen
became recognisable as vast jelly-forms. Hundreds and hundreds
of huge eggs pressed together, wobbling slightly in the current.

17

THE SPAWN

Where the bank grows steep and the willow fronds trail into the water, clouds of milky-coloured Spawn float, barely breaking the surface of the Pond where they part the layer of Green. They allow the Sun to filter through to the eggs and bathe them in a creamy haze.

The creatures now swam towards the Spawn, setting off just above Bear's Bucket. But they had not gone very far when they heard a strange threshing noise. Owen thought it sounded like a giant water-wheel or combine harvester.

"Keep down! It's the Moorhen, blurp," blustered the Rotifer.

"Hold on to something, everyone!" shouted Sedilla. "Owen, grab this weed frond. Take care you're not mown down."

Owen obeyed. Then, looking upwards through the turmoil, he saw two gigantic greeny-yellow claws thrashing through the water. They behaved just like a machine, cutting a way with their sharp paddle-blades. Behind each movement, little currents and eddies spun off into the surrounding water. Then the great machine disappeared as suddenly as it had come.

"That was a near thing," Bosmina gasped. "One thrash from those feet, and you'd be minced to shreds."

"I'm blurp, for going back, blurp. It's far too dangerous for the likes of me."

"Nonsense, we can't go back now. The eggs are just ahead. It would be a shame not to see them now we're here. I wouldn't miss them for anything."

"And it's our honeymoon treat," said Faluffel, "we wouldn't miss it for anything either."

"Oooh, look!" cried Charles. "Up there, straight ahead."

"How wonderful," squeaked Faluffel.

"How simply marvellous," sighed Daphnia.

"How superb," breathed Bosmina.

But the others, including Owen, were speechless.

As they approached, the milky film they had seen became recognisable as vast jelly-forms. Hundreds and hundreds of huge eggs pressed together, wobbling slightly in the current.

"Wow!" exclaimed Owen, pulling Sedilla along. "Faster, faster. I want to reach them."

"Hey," growled Ostracod. "Be quiet and sensible. In this bright light we are very vulnerable. No more talking from now on. We don't want our sound-waves to be detected. Grr."

"Yes, he's quite right," agreed Charles. "We must only make signs to one another." He put his arms around Faluffel, and quietly swam towards the jelly-eggs.

Soon they reached the outer banks of Spawn. The gelatinous edges formed cloud-shaped mounds, each one surrounded by a border of glowing light. On the underside of the banks where the Sun couldn't reach, the darkness pressed itself against the eggs. Owen left Sedilla and carried on. He felt this was a discovery he wanted to make alone. Everyone had the same feeling. Each wandered among the great eggs, awestruck with their beauty.

Owen swam towards the eggs where they began to slope out and break the surface. The round balls were larger than any Pond-bubble; thick in texture, glutinous and slightly opaque. He swam up close to one and touched its outside. The surface was sticky and slippery at the same time. Exactly in the middle of each egg was a black speck as big as himself, and each speck had a short tail. Owen felt exhilarated: it was an extraordinary sight, the best thing he had ever seen. He put his eye close to an egg, pressing his nose to the surface. He peered at the central black speck. "Tadpole," he whispered, "are you ready to come out yet?"

"No, no," came the reply as a tiny distant squeak. "Not ready yet. Not ready to come out yet."

Owen was disappointed. Surely some must be ready, he thought. I do so want to see just one hatching.

He decided to swim over to the adjoining mass of eggs. Maybe they would be further developed. Yes, the black specks and tails had grown slightly larger and, in addition, had minute arms. He asked one of these if it was ready to hatch.

"No, not quite ready. Not quite ready yet." came the distant reply. Owen swam round the edge of the mass, asking each one in turn, and although some said "Nearly ready" or "Very, very soon" none answered "Ready."

"Oh," said Owen sadly. "But this is probably the only time we'll be able to see you. Couldn't one of you just come out a little early?"

But although he pleaded, none would.

Exasperated, he decided to squeeze between the first two eggs and make his way into the middle of the mass. Perhaps one would be ready there. The eggs were very slippery, but he found he could displace them by pushing each sphere with both arms. They quickly became unstuck as he prised them apart, and then as quickly, stuck together behind him. As he squeezed past each one with its black speck, tail and limbs, he asked his question over and over again, but each time the weak cry answered in the negative. Faster and faster he forced his way through the wobbling mass of jelly. There were racks and racks of them above and below, but none were ready; and when he came to the other side of the mass, the cloud of eggs closed up behind, ejecting him into the surrounding water.

"Then I'll stay here until they hatch," he decided. "Sedilla will surely agree. I'll go and ask her."

Where were Sedilla, Bosmina, Daphnia and the others? He would go back and find them. Ostracod was bound to know how long he would have to wait before the Spawn hatched. He was swimming back to the first egg mass, when he spotted Daphnia ploughing towards him, a wild look in her eyes.

"Look out. Take care," she shouted, waving her feathery arms in panic. "A Stickleback is here."

Owen turned to see the enormous black shape cutting through the water. It was coming straight towards him.

The Stickleback could always be sure of a good meal or two from silly creatures who came to watch the Spawn. He had already eaten a foolish grub that morning, and here was another animalcule. He would eat some tadpoles too when they hatched.

Owen swam as he had never swum before. He forced himself through the water, making for the shadow under the Spawn. If he could press himself against the darkness he wouldn't be seen. He struck out harder as he looked back over his shoulder to see how near the Stickleback was.

To his surprise, the Stickleback had stopped following him. He had seen Daphnia and heard her shouting the warning to Owen. The great shark-like creature turned in a flash of orange-red underbelly, his three dorsal fins slicing the water, and made towards the plump form. His gaping mouth opened and shut at random, his gills pumped outwards and inwards, and his bulging eyes held a cruel gleam.

"Daphnia, look out. Look out!" Owen shouted, trying to attract the Stickleback's attention away from her. But although the fish flashed a look of electric blue towards him for an instant, Daphnia was nearer. He would eat her first. And Daphnia could not reach the safety of the Spawn. She tried to make for the huge weed-trunk behind, but her bulk slowed her down. The Stickleback darted forward, his tail cutting the water, his green body rolling slightly. He gave one snap in Daphnia's direction, and without so much as a pause to hear her plea ... gulped. His eyes remained unflinchingly open and his face did not change expression. Then he was gone. He had already seen something else to eat.

It was all over in a flash: but where Daphnia had been was now an empty space. There was no trace of her at all, not even an antenna.

"Daphnia, Daphnia, where are you?" Owen wailed through the water. "What's happened to you?"

"Disperse. Disperse and go home all of you," Sedilla screamed in panic, her voice rushing through the water in a series of rings before her agitated form appeared. "Quick, Owen. Find your Jar and hide. I'll see you later. Hurry."

She was in a complete frenzy, and before Owen could say anything, plunged downwards to warn Charles and Faluffel, and was soon out of sight.

Owen saw the retreating forms of Ostracod and Rottifer, swimming away in alarm. Soon they had all disappeared.

He stared aghast at the holes before him. From each one,
white teeth flashed and bright eyes glared back at him.
There were red ones, yellow ones, gleaming like head-lights ...

18

THE FURRY MONSTERS

After that, everything happened so fast and was so confusing that Owen was hardly able to take it in. At first he felt too frightened and weak to do anything but stay where he was, clinging to the lowest egg that hung down into the shadow. He decided to hide among the eggs until he could collect his senses, then swim for all he was worth back to his Jar. He had no idea where it was. As he pushed his way up through the egg-mass he formed a vague plan to go down to Bear's Bucket, perhaps to travel with someone back along the Ridge to the Centre; but for now, he was too shocked to do anything. Although he had seen death before, even Sedilla, whom he had thought lost forever, had recovered; but he had known deep in his heart that she would. There was no possibility of Daphnia 'recovering'. She had been eaten, and that was that. He needed time to Ponder it: sort it all out.

He realised he had taken Daphnia completely for granted. Now she wasn't around any more, he knew he was very fond of her. She had taught him how to swim; she had cried when Sedilla had died; she had warned him of the Stickleback, losing her own life in the process. He loved all the things that were Daphnia-like about her. Even her large size had been endearing. He had often been surprised at her greed, but she would have been completely different if she had been thin ... not like the Daphnia he knew. He should have shown his love for her much more when she was alive. He felt ashamed. Did one always feel this way after loved ones died? He resolved, from now on, to try and show his love for his friends. Not wait till they died or went away. This, he realised, had been the real reason why he hadn't any friends at school. It wasn't because he had been dim or goggle-eyed; it had been because he had spent the whole time worrying and feeling sorry for himself.

He thought about Daphnia as he made his way further and further up among the eggs. Had it been terrible for her to be eaten? He had been spat out before he reached the Salamander's stomach, but where had *she* got to now? Was she really inside the Stickleback as he swam along? Was she really already dissolved in his digestive juices? Ugh! The thought was appalling. And had the Stickleback enjoyed eating her? He certainly hadn't changed expression. In fact, he looked as though he had forgotten the whole experience the minute he swallowed her.

I'll have to talk to Sedilla about it when I get back, he thought.

Just then, he heard a loud booming noise. Then a colossal shadow loomed, obscuring the sunlight. He was shocked out of his Ponder. The Stickleback was obviously still in the vicinity, but the noise was coming from above. Was it a Moorhen or a bird – or perhaps Frogs coming to check on their Spawn? He climbed up and held onto an egg just below the surface, being careful not to touch the skin for fear of getting stuck. The huge shadow was above the surface, and something about the booming shape disturbed him. Something familiar awakened in him at the bellowing sound of the voice which, now he was just below the surface, had begun to make sense, forming itself into huge words, which he recognised as human speech.

"OWEN. OWEN, WHERE ARE YOU? THERE'S LOADS OF FROGSPAWN OVER HERE."

The large shape was hovering just above the bank of Spawn

to which Owen clung. How come Bethan was still here above the Green? Was Pond Time much faster than Human Time above?

"OH! HANG ON! THESE ARE NOT QUITE AS READY AS THE LOT I SAW FURTHER ROUND. I'LL GO BACK TO THEM. THEIR TAILS ARE MUCH LONGER."

The large shape was beginning to retreat, the voice drifting away.

"No. No, wait for me," shouted Owen, as loudly as he could. "Please take this Spawn, Bethan. I want to go home. They're nearly ready. They told me so themselves."

But it was useless. His voice was minute. Bethan couldn't possibly hear. There was only one thing to do, only one chance. He must swim round as fast as he could in the direction of her shadow and try to find the other Spawn she was looking for. It seemed to be going back towards the Shallows.

He let go the egg he was holding and pushed his way quickly to the edge of the stack. Then, half falling, half skidding down the slippery egg-surfaces to the shadow, he thrashed out fast through the open water.

He swam right across the Shallows, following the dark shadow easily through the clear water. As he swam, one image after another raced through his mind. First he thought of his Pond friends, saw Daphnia's death and the panic-stricken face of Sedilla shouting "Disperse, disperse." Then he saw his mother worrying at home; the school and the gang. Suddenly he wanted desperately to go back there above the Green. The Pond had its beautiful aspects. There were the bubbles and all his new friends ... but it was also treacherous, and life expectancy was terribly short.

The voice was now nowhere to be heard, the giant shadow become lost in the increasing darkness of water. Where was he?

Great brown cliffs of mud emerged through the murk. The

cliff-faces were pock-marked with scratches and scrabblings from clawed feet. Channels and passages had been drilled through the bank-side, huge holes loomed from under tangled roots and twisted willow stems.

Owen brought himself to a sudden halt with his emergency stop. He was terrified. He had come to the Edge! The very part that he and Sedilla had been so careful to avoid. No wonder they had seen no Spawn; it would have been hidden above the current, that sheet of swirling water. He stared aghast at the holes before him. From each one, white teeth flashed and bright eyes glared back at him. There were red ones, yellow ones, gleaming like head-lights ... and around them, darkness and silence.

"Furry Monsters!" Owen whispered to himself. "All of them."

Petrified, he started to back-tread quietly to the safety of the leaf of a huge Arrow-head plant, not daring to take his eyes off the piercing beams.

Why weren't they coming after him? Why weren't they devouring him? For one minute he thought they were frightened of him, but quickly dismissed the thought. Once again he heard Bethan's voice from above.

"THERE MIGHT BE EVEN MORE UNDER THIS WEED. COME OVER HERE, OWEN. PLEASE ANSWER ME. YOUR MOBILE ISN'T WORKING; IT JUST GAVE OUT A GURGLE."

"So that's it," thought Owen. "The Furry Monsters are as scared of Humans as I am of the Furry Monsters. No wonder I never caught a glimpse of one. They must have all plopped into the water when they heard Bethan's voice, and now they're cowering in their holes waiting for her to go. They won't dream of coming out while she's doing all that swirling about getting Spawn". Bethan had saved his life without even knowing it.

Owen realized it was imperative to follow Bethan's shadow or he'd be doomed. He swam very fast, keeping just a little way below the surface but with the Edge always in sight so he would always be under the protection of her shadow, taking care to avoid the bubbles coming from below, which he knew could be mortally dangerous. As he hurtled along, he saw all the Sticklebacks, Moorhens, Furry monsters and Salamanders hiding in the reeds, hollows and holes; all rigid with fear, all frozen with horror, while he, Owen, swam hard in view of them all.

Twice, when he thought he could go no further, the shadow paused, and he heard the voice right above him.

"I'VE GOT ENOUGH SPAWN NOW, OWEN, AND I'M GOING HOME WITHOUT YOU IF YOU DON'T SHOW YOURSELF SOON. WHY ARE YOU HIDING FROM ME?"

Owen realised that if Bethan left, all the Sticklebacks, Moorhens, Furry Monsters and Salamanders would emerge from hiding and pass the word round that it was safe. Then they would be after him like a shot. Some of the creatures he had seen looked *very* hungry.

"Don't go, Bethan," he implored uselessly.

He knew that once the shadow left, he would need to dive downwards as fast as possible to the Bottom and try to find the Ridge. Maybe he would find the others on their way back. Maybe they too had benefitted from the protection of Bethan's voice. He hoped so.

When he could no longer see the shadow, Owen dived deeply, not daring to risk going further. But as he slanted his way lower and lower, he could hear above him a terrible racket. It was as if a million Sticklebacks were snapping their jaws at once. A dreadful agitation followed, as if Furry Monsters were on the move. Currents strengthened, water whirled around with sediment disturbed from the Bottom. The view ahead was so turbid, it was practically impossible for him to see, and it got darker the further down he went.

When the Bottom was just beneath him, he started to swim along it, but the further he swam, the more he wondered whether he was even going in the right direction. There was now only one ambition in his mind; that was to reach the safety of his Jam-Jar Palace and shut the reed-entrance tightly behind him. But it was just like swimming through pea soup!

He began to feel trapped and exhausted in the stifling atmosphere. Dalyella the viridian Blob, the Planarian worms, the dreadful Dragonfly larvae; were they just in front? Could they detect him through the murk? He felt a wave of panic sweep over him. He was lost and alone. In complete despair, he shouted through the darkness: "Where am I and which way did I come this morning?"

"Why, you are exactly here, and the way you came this morning is exactly over there," said a voice he was sure was familiar. Then, just below, Owen recognised with pleasure the Caddis-fly larva, his case nicely completed with Owen's pencil cemented in place.

"Thanks," said Owen.

"Not at all. Any time. A pleasure to oblige. Pleasing, the rain, isn't it, after all this Sun?"

"Rain?" said Owen, puzzled.

"Yes, it's raining. You must be in a state not to have noticed. Mixes things up a bit, doesn't it?"

"Yes, I suppose so," said Owen. So that's what all the plopping noises and the terrible turbulence were.

"Very refreshing. Very refreshing for us all, indeed. Especially right down here where we need a mix up once in a while. Things can get a little too stagnant sometimes. Oh well, I shan't keep you. You're always in a hurry. Over there is where you came from," he said, pointing with his antennae. "And mind the Dragon-snappers. Goodbye."

Owen was overjoyed. Seeing the Caddis–fly larva meant he had avoided nearly all the creepy-crawlies below as well as the Furry Monsters of the Edge.

With renewed energy he hurried on, swimming slightly upwards over the rest of the Caddis larvae so that he would be too high for the Dragon-snappers.

After the snapping had died down behind him, Owen swam lower again, passing over the worms. These were wriggling excitedly, obviously loving the rain as it churned up food for them. The mud-banks were in a dreadful state, all heaved up and swilling round as sediment.

Swimming higher now, Owen found that the darkness was less intense and he was able to see the red area approach. The noise and turbulence had also abated, so he guessed it must have stopped raining for the time being. Once through the Ridge entrance with the red haze receding, Owen knew he was through the danger and had only to make his way uphill. He managed to turn sharp right at the place where Sedilla had turned sharp left that morning and, after a while, was passing over Lamellibranch the Mussel. But he was now too exhausted to greet him and carried on to Jam-Jar Palace. Stumbling in through the entrance, he blocked it tightly behind, then flung himself on the floor.

As Owen lay recovering, the murky water in the Jar turned pitch black so that he could see nothing. Then a great whoosh of sediment entered the Jar, and with it, such a commotion of water that he thought 'they' must have followed him back and were now coming in to eat him. But through the swirl he could see an enormously thick brown stick which wavered about for a while then was pushed under the rim of his Palace Jar to wrench it upwards at a precarious angle.

Owen lost his balance, tumbling and rolling to the far side of his Jar. The delicate reed entrance, which he had made so painstakingly, disintegrated as though it were made of paper; the reeds were wrenched away, letting in another great gush of water that spiralled round like a whirlpool. Then a gigantic pink hand reached in around the Jar, which started to travel upwards at an alarming rate. The force of the water was so strong that Owen was pressed flat against the base of his home, his arms and legs akimbo, his face turned sideways to avoid the full force of water.

Faster and faster they travelled. Owen felt himself being squeezed and squashed flatter and flatter. Waves of unconsciousness swept over him. Whilst around him the light grew brighter and a loud humming noise filled his ears with the pain of changing pressure. There was another jolt, followed by a feeling of lightness as the Jar was carried through the surface skin and beyond the green into the air.

"JUST WHAT I WANTED: ANOTHER JAR FOR MY EXTRA SPAWN. I'LL JUST CHUCK THIS MUDDY WATER AWAY AND GET SOME FRESH CLEAR WATER FOR THE SPAWN. THEN IT'S HOME FOR ME. IT'S STARTED RAINING AGAIN AND I'M GETTING SOAKED. OWEN MUST'VE GONE ON HOME WITHOUT ME."

Owen felt the jar tip as it was pulled sharply backwards and downwards. Then the direction changed with a jerk. Another great force lifted him and his murky surroundings spinning out of the jar, with a mighty whoosh. High in the air they sailed in an arc over the bank, over the thorn bushes; then landed with a 'plop' on the ground. With the violence of the landing, Owen blacked out.

He turned and looked at the Pond, then crept quietly
to sit by the edge. It was a soothing feeling as the rain fell
onto his hair and trickled down his face.

19

Metamorphosis

That was all Owen remembered of his journey out of the Green Pond, for when he came to, there was a searing pain in his chest and a violent panting noise at the back of his throat. He realised he was trying to breathe, but it was really hard as there seemed to be a lot of water in his chest. Then the pain spread over his whole body. It was a strange pain; a tingling that took hold of the extreme tips of his fingers down to the very ends of his toes. He was expanding! This must be what it was like to go through metamorphosis.

As his chest grew larger, Owen found it easier to breathe. He could take bigger gulps of air. The pain decreased and soon he was breathing normally. He unclenched his fists and finally opened his eyes.

There he was, Owen, full-sized. He sat up, took the glasses-case from the belt and opened it, letting the contents roll out.

My 5p coin, the paper-clip, my pencil and string are all missing, he thought. Then the memory of everything flooded back. Oh, of course, Sedilla has the 5p, Faluffel the clip and string, the Caddis-fly larva my pencil, and ... oh, he breathed in awe, I'm back again beyond the Green.

He stared round at the grass, then at the thorn bushes, whose spring buds were still unfurling into tiny delicate leaves. Through a gap in the thorn bushes, he could see the tiny figure of Bethan hurrying through the rain up the bank and into the wooded part, balancing a jam-jar of spawn in each hand.

He was about to get up and run after her when he looked down at himself. His socks, shoes and mobile, where were they? They must have been thrown out of the jar with him. Searching around he spotted them – his rolled up socks were stuck in a thorn bush, his shoes with the mobile wedged inside one of them in a soggy heap below.

Owen attempted to put his socks on but they wouldn't fit with his shoes, so he stuffed them in his pocket. Again he was about to run after Bethan, when something else stopped him. He didn't want to leave. He turned and looked at the Pond, then crept quietly to sit by the edge. It was a soothing feeling as the rain fell onto his hair and trickled down his face.

For a while Owen sat quite still, watching the Green seethe and churn in the rain. Small jets of water shot up as each raindrop hit the surface. The black cloud passed. The sun came out again, and the commotion on the surface ceased. A gentle wind blew up, ruffling the green water sideways into ripples. The rushes bent and waved at the side of the pond and a bird began to sing with a thin reedy voice from the branch of the willow tree. He heard a 'plop' and saw a small furry animal spring off the side of the bank sliding quickly through the water.

Owen turned and looked down. He had become aware of another presence. There, sure enough, keeping quite motionless on the stone beside him, was a salamander. For a moment their eyes met. Then the salamander gave him a look of utmost terror and, with a short whisk of his tail, hurtled through the air in a giant leap and splashed down into the pond.

"Thing!" shouted Owen after him. "Thing. Thing. Thing. Thing. Thing." And he rolled backwards onto the grass and laughed till the tears rolled down his face. Suddenly he felt very happy.

For a long while Owen watched, until the sun's rays went behind another dark cloud. The wind blew the willow branches more roughly so they skimmed through the water. He started to feel shivery and cold. The bird flew away. Now small rivulets of muddy water ran down the bank to join the pond. He got up to go, but his legs felt stiff and heavy and there was a strange feeling in his chest. Then he caught sight of a familiar pair of glasses-frames wedged between the roots of another thorn bush. He bent down and stared at them.

"These are my glasses, but I don't need them anymore. I can see as clearly now as I could below the Green Pond. How come? It must be some kind of Pond-miracle; a Pond-present; a way for me to completely change my life after everything I've learned." And he wrenched the horrid glasses from the thorn roots and flung them as far as he could towards the Shallows. "Perhaps the Pond creatures will find a use for them in there? Perhaps they will enjoy seeing Pond-life magnified through a shattered prism? Maybe the Pond Bear will use the prisms to make himself appear huge?"

His heart felt light as he walked homewards, but his body began to feel very hot and uncomfortable beneath the soggy clothes. He took his squelchy shoes off altogether, dropping his mobile into one of them, and carried them home.

"Owen, where have you been?" cried his mother, throwing up her hands. Her face looked tired and strained. "Bethan said she looked everywhere for you. Gracious, what a state you're in. What have you done to your clothes? They're completely water-logged right through to your skin. Your shoes," she said, looking down where he held them, "whyever are they off your feet? And your glasses," she said in horror, "you're not wearing any! How did you manage to get home without them? Why, Owen, you're boiling hot. Your forehead is ablaze with fever. Go straight to bed while I ring for the doctor. No, don't start on about the pond. Just do as I say."

As Owen struggled upstairs, Bethan came out of her room. "There you are, Owen. I searched for you everywhere. Oh, Owen, you didn't fall in, did you?" Bethan laughed. "No wonder I couldn't find you anywhere. No wonder your mobile went dead." But then she saw that her twin brother looked very strange – entirely different.

Owen did not know when the doctor came, for as soon as he reached his room, he collapsed onto his bed.

The days passed. Owen tossed and turned, raging with fever. He was heard to mutter strange things. He warned people of Pond-ghosts, told them not to go near the Edge or the Furry Monsters would get them. He cried out too for someone called Sedilla. No-one could make head or tail of any of it. They thought he might have gone out of his mind.

"Owen, Owen," his mother was calling him. Owen opened his eyes. His mother was bending over him. Behind her, his father was standing nervously, looking anxious and concerned. "Do you feel better now, son?" he enquired.

"Look, Owen," said Bethan, "I've brought you these. She placed a jam-jar … his own 'Green Giant' jam-jar, on the window-sill where the sun shone through the glass.

"Don't chat to him for too long, dear," his mother interrupted, as she turned and shut the door, quietly following his father downstairs. "There are some pancakes for you both to have later, in the kitchen."

"I brought some of the spawn back from school. I thought you might want to watch them. They're just about to hatch. I've got some on my own window-sill to look at."

"Thanks, Bethan," Owen said. "They're ready now. Ready to come out," he murmured gently, almost to himself.

"In a few days, if you're better enough, we'll go and release the tadpoles back into the pond."

"You know, Bethan, I thought we knew everything about our secret pond, but we don't really. And I'm definitely going to become 'A World's Expert' on everything that happens below Ponds – find out completely how Pond Life works ... though I know quite a lot about it already."

Bethan smiled at him. "You know, everyone at school missed you not being there. They've all been saying things like "Wow! Fancy Owen having pneumonia. Cool! " I think you'll find you're quite a star when you get back. Can you really see without your glasses?"

"Yes," said Owen, "perfectly well. I'll never need them again."

"It must have been that fever, I suppose ... a magic kind of fever to restore your sight like that."

Bethan stood by the jar of frogspawn and scrutinised her brother carefully. "Well I think you look ever so much nicer without them."

Glossary

Note: The Pond Creatures in this book are based on fact, with names as close as possible to their species names, but for the purpose of this story, two facts have been modified: characters such as Ostracod and Rottifer are presented as male, though most creatures are female or hermaphrodite; all water-fleas are one-eyed – not just Cyclops.

Pond Characters – Latin Names
Amoeba – Amoeba proteus
Bosmina – Bosmina longirostris
Charles Copepod – Calanoid copepod
Cristatella – Cristatella mucedo
Cyclops – Cyclops strenuus
Dalyella Viridis – Dalyella viridis
Daphnia – Daphnia magna
Difflugia – Difflugia
Diplodontus Despiciens – Diplodontus despiciens
Dugesia Lugubris – Dugesia lugubris
Euglena Flagellata – Euglena flagellata
Faluffel – Daphnia longispina
Fluke – Diplozoon paradoxum
Fredericella Sultana – Fredericella sultana
Geoffroy – Corixa geoffroyi
Glossosiphonia Complanata – Glossosiphonia complanata
Gnat Larva – Sitnulium
Gordius – Gordius aquaticus
Great Pond Snail – Limnaea stagnalis
Grisella – Daphnia cucullata
Heliozoa – Heliozoa
Hermione the Hydra Witch – Hydra chlorohydra viridis
Lamellibranch – Anodonta cygnea (lamellibranchia)
Mesostoma – Mesostoma tetragonum
Moorhen – Gallinula chloropus

Mosquito Wiggler – Culex pipiens
Mysis Relicta Shrimps – Mysis relicta
Neta – Argyroneta aquatica
Ostracod – Ostracod cypris reptans
Owen – Homo sapiens
Plumatella Fungosa – Plumatella fungosa
Pond Bear – Sigismund tardigrada
Pond Sponge – Espongilla lacustris
Raft Spider – Dolmedes fimbriatus
Rat-tailed Maggot – Tubifera
Red Worm – Tubifex tubifex
Rottifer – Rotifer rotaria rotatoria
Salamander – Triturus cristatus
Sedilla – Sida crystallina
Slipper-animalcule – Paramecium
Springtail – Podura aquatica
Stickleback – Gasterosteus
Victorella – Victorella
Volvox – Volvox
Water Hog-Louse – Asellus aquaticus (isopod)
Water Shrew – Neomys fodiens
Water Strider – Gerris najas
Water Vole – Arvicola terrestris
Whirligig Beetle – Gyrinus natator

If you have enjoyed this book and would like to find out more about pondlife, here are some suggestions for further reading:

Allen, Gwen and Denslow, Joan. *'Freshwater animals'.* Oxford University Press 1970.

Burton, Robert. *'Ponds: Their Wildlife and Upkeep'.* David and Charles, 1977.

Clegg, John. *'Freshwater Life of the British Isles'.* Frederick Warne, 1974.

Clegg, John. *'The Observer's Book of Pond Life'.* Frederick Warne, 2nd edition, 1967.

Garnett, W. J. *'Freshwater Microscopy'.* Constable, 1965.

Leutscher, Alfred. *'Life in Fresh Waters'.* Bodley Head, 1964.

Silverstein, Alvin and Virginia. *'A world in a Drop of Water'.* Blackie, 1970.